MW01234158

PLAYING CAT AND MOUSE

THE CELTIC WITCH MYSTERIES

BOOK TWO

Molly Milligan

Text copyright 2017 Molly Milligan
All Rights Reserved
This is a work of fiction

ONE

Just before Gwyl Canol Gwenwynol – spring equinox – mid-March

I could cope with the rabbits all over the place, but the chocolate?

So. Much. *Chocolate.*

I leaned against the grey wall and very deliberately cast my eyes upwards to the not-quite-wintery sky. I did not want to look across the street at the tempting window display of the shop opposite. Somewhere, I could hear a distant argument between a man and a woman taking place on the street. I ignored it.

Chocolate, chocolate, chocolate. My stomach rumbled.

Come on, I willed. My Great Aunt Dilys was shopping and I had elected to wait outside this particular place. It was a new age mystical shop that leaned towards the tackier end of the spectrum. And when I say "leaned" I suppose I mean "falls face down into it, laughing about rainbows." It's not that I have anything against magical things – and wow, Sian Pederi sold a ton of the stuff – but my magic is a more homely sort. I'm a hedge witch. If I have a spare five pound note, I'll spend it on cakes and food for my animals, not a greetings card with a multi-coloured glittery fairy on it. All their legs seem too long, anyway.

But it was approaching an early Easter in our small Welsh town. It didn't matter if you were "chapel" or "Church in Wales" or "Jedi" or "witch" or "none of the above" – in spite of the crucifixion posters in some people's windows, mostly this time of year meant chocolate in profusion. Eggs, rabbits, whatever.

Unfortunately my American cousin Maddie had decided this was the right time to try and persuade me to "eat a little cleaner" which apparently meant "birdseed and vegetable peelings." Not a lot of chocolate featured in her recipe ideas.

I was actually doing pretty well in sticking to Maddie's colour-coded meal plan, but it was hard. I kept my eyes on the blue-grey sky above the row of shops, and sighed. Dilys was probably reading someone's fortune in Sian's shop. I was a healer and I often got waylaid when I was out and about, by people asking for help for themselves or their animals. My aunt, meanwhile, was a seer and she got stopped by people who wanted to know their futures.

I huffed, and turned to peer in through the window. I could just make out the shadowy shape of my diminutive aunt, and she did indeed appear to be reading someone's palm. Knowing her, she could be in there for some time.

Then I got a call from my cat, a plaintive cry for assistance that shot directly into my brain, and my mind was made up. I'd have to leave Dilys to her fortune telling, and return home to deal with whatever injured animal Harkin had brought to me for healing. It was a great excuse to get away and I wanted to get home to carry on with the tasks piling up for me. I cracked open the door to the shop, and nearly choked with the smell of incense. I didn't disturb my aunt but I waved at Sian who was behind the counter, and mouthed, "I'm going home", nodding at my aunt's back. I hoped that conveyed my meaning. Sian nodded, anyway, and the feathers in her pink hair danced and wafted like a peacock doing a mating ritual.

I left the shop and began walking across the street, heading for the market square. I let Harkin into my mind again, trying to work out what the cat was telling me. He couldn't use words but he was good at sending impressions, and sometimes even rough images, though what a cat sees and what we see are quite different.

I was getting a feeling of sharpness and indignation. A hedgehog, then. And there was a fleeting moment of tightness around my neck. I suspected it would be a hedgehog trapped in something – likely either an illegal snare, or one of those plastic beer can ring holder things. I quickened my pace. Harkin wasn't sending me any feelings of desperation, but it had been a few hours since I'd had a cup of tea and my mouth was dry, so getting home seemed like a good idea anyway.

"Watch out, you stupid old biddy! You blind or what, eh?"

That shout that came from behind me was so rough and loud that I stopped. Everyone turned to see the man who was making a scene. I spun around, too, and my heart stopped for a moment.

There was my aunt, her hands in the air as if she was warding someone off, and at her feet was all her shopping, scattered around. She'd obviously left the shop a moment after I had. Behind her, Sian came out of her shop, and began to pick up some of the tins that were rolling on the pavement.

But my attention focussed on the man who was shaking his fist at Great Aunt Dilys. I'd seen him in passing over the past few weeks, a big man and new to the town, so he stood out. He was English, too, and his loud voice carried across the square as he yelled.

"You ought to be put in a home!" he roared at my aunt. *My aunt! How dare he!*

Although I didn't really know the angry man properly, I knew the slim, pretty woman with the wavy blonde hair who was standing a few paces behind him. That was Chloe Davies, adult daughter of a local farming family, and she was looking acutely embarrassed about the whole thing.

Embarrassed? My fury rose. *I'd show her 'embarrassed'!*

I ran across the street, causing a lad on a moped to skid around me and swear through his flipped-up helmet. I showed him my middle finger – yeah, I know, I am *such* a lady – and descended on the English man, my hands clenched.

I stopped a few feet away. "Don't you dare speak to my aunt like that!" I spat.

Up close, he was a lot bigger. And wider. His girlfriend, Chloe, took three more steps away from us. It dawned on me that no one was exactly leaping to my aid. I tried to make myself tall.

He narrowed his eyes at me, and every inch of his handsome face was made ugly as he said, "She ain't fit to be out on her own. Crap niece you are, aren't you, letting some poor old lady roam about. Don't you think you ought to help her with her shopping? I wouldn't treat a member of my family like that."

Hang on. How did this end up about me? Sian had taken Great Aunt Dilys to one side and was checking she was okay. I saw, out of the corner of my eye, my cousin Maddie appear. She helped out in Sian's shop, now, and must have been in the back room earlier.

I was just about to turn away from the horrible man. I couldn't win a fist-fight against him. In truth I probably couldn't win a fist-fight against a pillow. I heard him say to Chloe, "What is wrong with the dumb people in your town?" He was half-turning from me, too, and as he did so, he kicked out and caught a packet of biscuits that had spilled from my aunt's shopping bags. They tumbled into the gutter and were promptly flattened, run over by a passing car.

"Hey! You owe us a pack of biscuits!" I blurted out.

He sneered at me. "You what? I don't think so, *darling*."

Finally, Chloe spoke up.

She didn't address her hulking brute of a boyfriend, though. Instead she turned her watery eyes on me, and said, "Bronwen, Bronnie, leave it … David doesn't really mean it."

I am not *Bronnie*, not to anyone. Now I was really annoyed. "Don't tell *me* to leave it! Tell him, the bully." I pointed at that David. He grabbed hold of Chloe's arm and made her squeal. She stayed rigid as he pulled her to his side.

"You leave my Chloe out of this," he snarled.

"I never brought her into it. She has a mind of her own anyway."

Maddie forced her way in between us, then, with her arms straight out either side, holding us apart like the referee in a boxing match.

"No, Maddie, don't!" I said.

But she did. She unleashed her glamour and I could see, from the corners of my eyes, the sparkling lights that heralded the duplicitous, tricksy arrival of the Tylwyth Teg, the Fair Folk, the glamourous and untrustworthy Faerie themselves.

"Bron," she said to me, smiling. "Our Aunt Dilys needs you." Then she cocked her head towards the rude man, and I knew, without being able to see her face, that she would be fixing him with her green eyes. "Now, sir, I am sure that this has blown out of all proportion and we'd all really like to go home and have a nice cup of tea."

I nearly laughed. It was funny to hear her American vowels crooning out such a British thing to say. And really, the facts of the sentence were the least important thing. She used her Faerie-learned glamour, and that is what made the man shudder all over, like a wet dog, and step back from her.

"Yeah, well, just watch out, all right?" he muttered but his malice was gone. He grabbed hold of Chloe again, and half-dragged her away down the street.

Maddie bent to start picking up the rest of the scattered groceries. Often the use of glamour took its toll on her, but that had been a short and light blast, and she didn't seem too affected.

"I can't believe that man!" I burst out.

"Help me pick up this stuff," she said calmly, humming to herself under her breath, a new habit that I recognised as her way of thanking the Faeries for their aid.

"I can't believe that woman, either! That Chloe! She learned no decent manners while she's been away wherever it is. London. Cardiff. Somewhere busy and smelly. She just stood by and did nothing while he bullied my aunt, and me!"

"Help me pick up this stuff," Maddie repeated. She was crouching down and she glared up at me.

"Don't you try your glamour on me," I said.

She shot to her feet and grabbed my arm. "I'm not. I wouldn't. Stop complaining and get on with actually being useful, you know? Pick up the stuff. Or, maybe, you might wanna see to Dilys?"

I wanted to pick up a can of beans and hurl it at the back of the man's head. I am proud to say that I restrained myself, and instead took a deep breath and went to check that Dilys was all right.

"Fine, fine, give over now," Dilys said, as she came forward, pushed past me, and helped Maddie pick up the last few items. A few onlookers tutted in the direction that the man and Chloe had gone, which counts as a pretty strong show of support for me here, to be honest. It was a very British disapproval.

"So, who was he?" Maddie said. "Come on, I'll come home with you. That okay, Sian?"

Sian nodded and retreated into her shop. I was aware that Harkin was still calling for me. Maddie and I picked up the

9

various bags and we positioned Dilys in between us. It did mean we took up all the pavement like a gang on the prowl, but I was feeling belligerent and I didn't care.

"Seriously, Maddie, I appreciate the peacekeeping and all that, but you should have let me smack that guy," I said. "Chloe, his girlfriend, grew up here. I don't know what they're doing but someone said they'd moved back here for good. You should have let me put him in his place. He can't be allowed to think he can get away with that sort of thing. It's not how we are. Not in Llanfair."

"He was getting more and more angry," she pointed out.

"I don't care. Okay so I couldn't punch him. But I could have bitten his nose off or something. Maybe hexed him. Hey, I still can do that. Let me get home and…"

"No. Don't you see? That poor girl Chloe is afraid of him. If he can't take it out on you, he will just take it out on her, later."

A cold finger stroked down the back of my neck. "Then why on earth does she stay with him?"

Dilys sighed heavily and I could tell that Maddie was exasperated with me, too, just from the tone of her voice as she said, "Bron, I love you very much but you are an idiot. Things are never so black and white, you know?"

We passed the last few shops and now we were walking along a narrower path that led out to where our old house stood. I fell behind to allow Maddie to walk alongside Dilys. They supported one another. I heard Dilys say something about an upcoming Mind, Body and Spirit Fair, and Maddie said something reassuring in return. I didn't even know which one they were referring to.

"I was going to do it in the shop," Maddie said to Dilys. "We'll have to do it tonight now."

"What about her?"

Maddie seemed to half look back at me.

Were they talking about me?

"Hey," I said, starting forward and shoving myself between them.

If things weren't black and white, I told myself crossly, then they ought to be.

And yet my life and my magical practise was all to do with boundaries and edges and the grey areas.

I felt a greyness stalking me all the way home.

TWO

Nothing exciting happened at all the rest of the day – once I'd sorted out the animal that Harkin had called me for (yes, an injured hedgehog, and yes, it was caught in a twist of plastic, and no, it wasn't serious as I had caught it early enough).

And nice and calm is exactly how I like it. Not exciting, not alarming, not unusual in any way. Since I'd discovered a dead body in the undergrowth of our garden a few months earlier, Maddie had been harbouring fantasies that we'd become some mystery-solving team, but I was perfectly content to stay as a small-town healer. I would do some gardening, and go for long hikes, and meditate, and make jam. Life, lived small, can be good. That was my motto.

Maddie didn't live small. It's not that she was the stereotype of loud, effusive American (although she kinda was, I suppose) but she was naturally warm and her heart was simply too large to be restrained in a small and narrow existence. And she liked to meddle, too, though she painted it as "improving the lives of those I love" – hence the healthy food.

I know she was a good example to me, and from time to

time I thought I ought to be more like her.

She was always cheerful.

So it was a surprise when I went downstairs the next morning to find a sombre mood in the kitchen. Dilys was standing by the range, threatening the kettle unless it boiled faster. (I am not sure what she was threatening it with. What are kettles scared of? Rusty bottoms?) Maddie sat at the long, scrubbed table. It would have been the very picture of chic farmhouse style, were it not for the fact that it was overflowing with actual mess and everyday clutter. There were piles of newspapers in Welsh and English, a tin whistle, three pairs of thermal socks, half a bag of birdseed clipped firmly closed with a plastic thing, some knitting yarn, and Maddie's iPad propped up on a chipped china shepherdess.

She was slumped in her chair and staring at the screen, chewing her lip. As soon as she saw me enter the room, though, she straightened up and plastered a smile onto her face.

"Hey hey," she trilled. "It's my favourite cousin and Llanfair's local peacekeeping force, Bron!"

"Llanfair," I said, stressing the "ll".

"That is exactly what I said," she retorted.

It was not. But I grinned because she'd tried to make the impossible Welsh "ll" sound. (Just imagine you're huskily breathing an "l" while your tongue is lodged against the roof of your mouth and you blow out the sides of your lips. It's just like that. Nearly. But spittier.)

I was curious about the iPad. I glanced at the screen as I went behind Maddie to get to the range, where I joined my aunt in staring at the kettle. Behind me, the iPad started to make a high-pitched squealing noise. I damped down my natural anti-technology energy as much as I could, but it was no use.

Maddie sighed heavily and pressed a button on it until the noise stopped. I turned around. The screen had gone dark and so had her expression.

"What's up?" I said. "Don't you usually go to the library to do your internet things?"

"Yeah." She slumped in the seat.

I felt acutely sorry for her. My hedge witch powers bring both blessings and curses – the main problem being that I am allergic to technology. Or, perhaps it's more accurate to say that technology is allergic to me. I blow fuses and I make electronics go haywire. I don't own a mobile phone and our house has limited gadgets. The electricity is well-shielded from me, but there are limits. And we certainly don't have wi-fi.

"I just wanted to Skype my mom and dad," she said forlornly. "I thought it might work while you were upstairs."

"Did it? I can go away again."

"No," she said. "It didn't. I just feel a little homesick, you know?" She shook herself and straightened up. "I guess I'll go visit the library later. It's just kinda weird talking to mom in a public place. Ha, I spend so long in the library, they'll be charging me rent soon. You guys totally need to get a MacDonald's built here. Not for the food, you know. Just so I can sit out in the parking lot and use the wi-fi."

Finally the kettle had boiled. Dilys swilled the big teapot with some hot water and then filled it right up with fresh water.

She plonked it onto the table and covered it with a garishly-knitted cosy. "Don't fret yourself," she said to Maddie. "You do get used to it."

Maddie smiled weakly.

I realised, with a sick jolt, that she wasn't talking about homesickness. I looked again at my aunt who seemed oblivious to my scrutiny. I supposed that Dilys had had to get used to living with me and all the restrictions that my curse brought.

I hadn't really thought about that before.

***

After breakfast I invited Maddie out on a walk with me. "Look, it's starting to snow!" I said.

She rushed to the window and jumped up and down with glee. "Finally!"

I'd been promising her snow for weeks now. She'd arrived in Britain in early February and I think she'd expected us to be knee-deep in the stuff like on Christmas cards. She did so much for me that I had made a vow to myself to be a better person for her, too. Even though I had other work to do, I took the time now to go out into the snow with her because I knew it would delight her.

We togged ourselves up in many layers of sensible outdoor gear and headed out to visit Gruffydd, the blacksmith, and a good friend of mine. Thin white flakes spiralled slowly from the leaden grey clouds above us. It wasn't much of a snowstorm and it didn't look likely to settle very thickly.

But it was still snow. Maddie in particular was beside herself with joy. "It literally does *not* snow in my part of California!" she declared as she danced along the path. "I mean, it might fall a little, once in a blue moon, but it doesn't stick, and it's like, front page news and all. Whee!"

"Hey," I said as we scuffed our feet through the thin layer on the path. "I really am sorry about the internet and the computer and all the problems that I cause."

She linked her arm into mine, but after three steps we'd both lost our balance so she had to relinquish her grip. "It's fine," she assured me. "Don't sweat it, okay?"

"But I-"

"Hush now!"

"Thanks. How is the work with the Faeries going?"

"Hard. Interesting, challenging. I have to be on my guard."

"I worry," I said. "You use glamour on others, but how do you know whether to trust them?"

"We have made a pact," she said. "You can't trust them, but I can, because of my bond with them."

"But what if it's all a trick?"

She sighed. "What if everything is a trick? Love? Life? We will never really know until the end. Sometimes you just gotta step off the ledge, you know? Ah, look at that. Some new store opening up, do you think?"

We had reached the outskirts of the town centre now and she obviously wanted to change the subject. The road was still clear of snow due to the traffic cutting a path through it but the pavement was becoming slippery. I followed her finger and saw that a once-boarded-up shop was now all lit up, and the plywood had been removed to reveal a big plate-glass window. There was no sign above the door yet, but we could see quite clearly inside.

"Oh, god, it's that man again," I muttered. "Chloe's boyfriend. David something or other. David Big-Rude-Bully."

"Who is that other man? He looks kinda lost. He doesn't fit in there."

We worked our way closer but stayed on the far side of the road, half-hidden by a parked car. "Oh, that's just Edmund Tait. He's a farmer."

"I would never have guessed. Not with the coveralls and boots and hat and all," Maddie said.

The interior of the shop was all bright and clean. There were two long desks and some expensive-looking computer hardware there. I couldn't imagine what the business was going to operate as. Chloe was sitting on the edge of a desk, swinging her long stockinged legs, looking at a clipboard in her hands. Her boyfriend Mr Big-Rude-Bully was standing with his arms folded, and he was talking with Tait, who was slightly hunch-backed and had his head partly angled away. If he had been a dog, his tail would have been between his legs.

But Mr Big-Rude-Bully wasn't talking angrily and his face was open and friendly. So quite why Tait looked so cowed was a mystery.

We moved on before we could be spotted lurking behind the car. Maddie wanted to stop and call in at the best café in town, Caffi Cwtch. It was run by a man called Alston, for whom the word "curmudgeon" had been invented. When we looked in, we saw that the place was full and every table was taken – in spite of his horrible demeanour, he made the best cakes in Llanfair. And, to Maddie's delight, he also created amazing fruit sorbets, ices, salads and smoothies. We both knew these things were brimming with sugar, but because they had the word "fruit" near to them, we could kid ourselves that they were the healthy option.

Yeah, eating clean …? It was a nice idea.

Anyway, the café was too crowded so we continued out of town along a narrow road that led to Gruffydd's forge. Again we were thwarted. We were about two hundred yards from his place when a pickup truck rattled past, coming from the direction we were heading in and going to town, and the cheery face of Gruffydd grinned at us from the window.

We waved past, and stopped.

"Well, this whole walk was a waste of time," I said.

"Aw, come on," Maddie said, bumping me with her elbow. "I only really wanted to see snow, and I have seen snow! You know, it's snowing a whole lot more now. Let's keep on walking. I wanna see what it's like up in the hills."

"Cold," I said, grumpily. "That is what it is like. Really cold."

"Nah, I'd say bracing. Exhilarating. Life-affirming, you know? Indulge me, Bron! I need to see snow, right?"

I sighed, and nodded. "All right, then. Let's go."

We were very lucky to live in such a rural area of Wales. We followed the track past Gruffydd's forge and soon it petered out into a mere path as we passed a lonely farm. Now the land rose up steeply.

This was my land, and the source of my power as a hedge rider. I breathed in deeply. Maddie was right. It was exhilarating.

The snow was falling more thickly now. I didn't want to lead us astray so when we came to a fork in the path, I took the route that went along the side of the hill. It wouldn't have been wise to continue to climb higher.

We would have had a good view of the town from here, but the snow cut us off. Even the path was becoming harder to follow. I aimed for a stone wall and we followed that.

Our feet slipped on the snow-covered rocks and my nose was getting very cold. Exhilarating? Yeah, right. My enthusiasm for the walk had long since gone and it didn't seem like it was going to come back.

"What's so funny?" Maddie said. She was trying to re-tie her scarf around her nose, and she looked frozen.

"Nothing," I said. "I was just thinking that I wanted to walk, then I didn't want to walk, then I did, and now I don't again."

"Time of the month?" she offered.

"Time for a hot cup of tea," I replied. "Come on. If we keep going this way, we'll see a path on our right that will bring us out at the back of the church. We can cut through the churchyard and over the wall into our garden."

We ploughed on, chatting about nothing much. I didn't mention her Faerie work again. I did suppose she was right – though I couldn't trust them, she could. After all, though I rode the hedge, that didn't mean anyone could safely walk the corpse roads and I certainly wouldn't encourage it.

At times, the snow was so thick that we could barely see

anything, and we had to stop. I would close my eyes and feel my way by thought, checking that we were still on the right route. I had never ever been lost in my entire life. I couldn't find my way to new places like this, but I could always, without fail, get home. I had been born in that house and there was a tie to me that could not break. I let my awareness rise up, onto the corpse roads, just lightly, and from there I could almost see – like out of the corners of my eyes, though they were still closed – the patterns of the hills that were so familiar to me. And a thread that connected me to the house my family had always lived in, for generations lost to time.

We were going in the right direction. Now the snow was four inches thick on the ground. "This wasn't forecast," Maddie said. "But hey, it's cool."

"Cold, more like."

"Ha ha. Hey, what's that? Up ahead, do you see it?"

I strained my eyes. The snow came in flurries rather than a solid sheet of flakes, and as the wind eddied around us, I caught a glimpse of blue flashing lights.

There is something about such a thing that makes everyone's blood run cold.

We started forward again, hurrying now. I didn't bother to try to follow the right path. We just made straight for the lights, and as we got closer we could see orange and yellow clothing, and hear voices, mostly English words with Welsh accents.

"Oh my gosh," Maddie said. "Something really has happened. This can't be good, right?"

I felt ill, and I am sure that she did, too. We couldn't make out the scene properly until we were nearly upon it. There were three men kneeling around something on the ground, and a four-wheel-drive vehicle parked up a little way below us, its lights flashing. Someone else was on a walkie-talkie, and when he turned around I saw that it was Adam.

Adam is a local policeman, and my boyfriend, mostly. Well, we date. It's fun. But with his unsocial shifts, and my antipathy to technology, things can get a little difficult.

He waved at us, grimly, and finished his call before hurrying over to us, neatly steering us away from the huddle of high-vis people. I could see that they were putting something – no, someone – onto an orange plastic stretcher.

"What's happening?" Maddie and I asked in unison, more like twins than cousins.

"Someone has fallen," he said. "They are badly hurt and we need to get them down off the hill. What on earth are you guys doing up here? It's a long way to come rubber-necking."

"Just walking." I ignored the tone of disapproval in his voice.

He looked at us like we were crazy. Which was fair enough. "In this weather?"

"Well, it wasn't this bad when we left. Anyway, we are nearly home."

"You've got over a mile yet just to get onto the road."

I shrugged.

He shook his head, but his attention wasn't fully on us. "Look, are you going to be okay getting home? I'd see you home, but I just need to deal with this. And you both need to get away from here."

"Sure," Maddie said and I agreed.

"Go and help the walker," I said.

"It's not a walker," Adam said as he pulled his walkie-talkie free of the clip on his belt again. "It's some random businessman from the town. I have no idea what he was doing up here, or how he came to have fallen and taken such an impact."

"Businessman?"

"David Hudson, some new chap from London, they reckon."

One of the mountain rescue team gave a yell and began to beckon Adam over.

We took a few steps back, and turned around, and headed for home as quickly as we could.

THREE

"Death," said Dilys in a satisfied tone as she stared into the dregs of tea she'd poured from her cup into the saucer.

I met Maddie's eyes and we both shivered. We'd got home late, tired and hungry, and only briefly mentioned the escapade on the hills. Now it was the morning after, and I had been wondering how the injured man was faring. Although as it was that bully David Hudson, I thought I might pay him in a visit in hospital, take him some grapes, and then just sit at the end of the bed and eat them all without offering him any. I am not a malicious person, but the idea of being a little petty did appeal to me.

Still, I did draw the line at wishing death upon anyone.

"Whose death?" I queried, keeping my tone light, as if it were a perfectly normal conversation to be having.

"Oh, not mine," she assured me.

"I didn't think it would be," I said. "You're not that old, really."

"I am ancient, and fit only for compost," Dilys said in a calm voice. "I am staying alive out of sheer stubbornness. Mabel said I'd go before her, and so I shan't."

Maddie wrapped her arms around herself and went to the window. It was cold even in the usually-warm kitchen, and she was wearing a thick jumper and a bodywarmer. Or, in her strange-yet-familiar language, a turtle-neck sweater and a padded gilet or vest.

"It's still snowing," she said. "Man, it's a white-out out there."

"You wanted snow," I pointed out. "It's probably your fault." I didn't think she could change the weather, even with the help of her Faerie friends. But who knew for sure?

"Yeah, I wanted snow," she admitted. "But kinda warmer?"

"Er, that's not how snow works."

"I went skiing up June Lake one time," she said. "I don't remember it being so cold like this. Oh! Here comes Adam." She shot me a sideways look and grinned.

"Shwmae," he said as he came in through the back door and through the small utility room on the back of the house. It housed all the sick and injured animals that I cared for, as well as about thirteen odd wellington boots, various coats, the washing machine, a stone sink that was heavier than a small family car, some unlabelled mystery tins, and a pervasive odd smell.

"Shwmae," Maddie said in return.

Both Dilys and I sighed and smiled. It was always funny to hear non-Welsh people try to speak Welsh. Adam had grown up in Zambia and mangled our lovely language in a wonderful way. Maddie's accent was no better, but she was also trying to learn

Welsh.

I was slightly afraid that she'd get better than I was at the language. I'd learned it at school, but that differed from the everyday mix of English and rough Welsh that we spoke in the town. I wasn't fluent, not by a long way. Although I could still say "ll" better than she could.

"What news on that guy from yesterday?" Maddie asked as I waved Adam into a chair and offered him a cup of tea.

He was in his uniform, and on duty. He refused the brew, and assumed a sombre expression. "Bad news, I'm afraid."

We all knew instantly what he meant. "He's dead, isn't he?"

"Yes. He passed away in the night due to the extent of his injuries. He had a massive bleed on the brain."

We all paused for a moment in silence.

"Anyway, that's not why I'm here," Adam said. "I just wanted to check you were all right. I tried to call you, but all the phone lines are down."

And it's not like a mobile phone is of any use here, I thought bitterly. *My curse really does affect people around me, not just me alone.*

No one else seemed bothered about the phones, though. Maddie was thanking him for his attention, and assuring him that we got home without mishap. "But what about that guy, though?" she asked. "His family must be devastated."

"They have been informed."

I thought of Chloe. Surely she'd be ultimately better off without such a bully? Not that I would wish the man to die, of course. But just, you know, maybe he could have got a really bad stomach ache and maybe some diarrhoea and gone off to live

27

somewhere else. And regardless of how he treated her, no doubt she'd be upset. I resolved to continue to be a better person, and go to offer my support.

"The thing is," Maddie said, chewing her lip. "It's a bit strange, you know? Why was he up there in the snowstorm? We saw him earlier yesterday. And not, like, much earlier. Maybe an hour, tops? What do you think, Bron?"

"We walked up from town past Gruffydd's place … yeah, that would be just over an hour, an hour and a half what with the snow."

"Where did you see him?" Adam asked, putting his proper-policing expression on his face, all thin mouth and calm eyebrows.

"In the new business that's opening up on the main street. I assume it was something to do with him. I don't know what they're going to do, but he was in there with Chloe and that farmer, Edmund Tait. Are they offering some kind of agricultural service?" I said, with no idea at all as to what that service might be. Rent-a-tractor?

"Oh, I think they intend to do graphics and stuff, advertising for businesses, and maybe websites," Adam said. "I don't know why Tait would want one. He doesn't have his own farm, anyway. He works for Twm."

"That's right," I said, remembering then that Twm and his twin ran a large flock of sheep. "But Chloe is from a farming family and they are about the same age. They're probably just friends. They'll have been to all the same Young Farmers' balls together. You haven't answered Maddie's question, though. Why was he on the hill in the snow?"

"Nobody knows. We spoke with Chloe and she told us that he'd been there in the place you saw him, with Tait, and then he'd left. He hadn't said that he was going for a walk. He wasn't dressed for walking. And his injuries were quite severe. It is a mystery."

Maddie was making eye contact with me and I knew why. As soon as I met her gaze, she burst out, "Foul play! Someone beat him up, right?"

"No," Adam said. "Actually he looked very much like he'd fallen, at speed, from a height."

"A cliff?"

"It looked like it, but there is nothing there that he could have fallen from. He was in the middle of an empty field."

"Then how?"

Adam lowered his voice. "Keep this to yourselves for the moment. Basically, the accident investigators have said he must have fallen from a quad bike. After all, most of the farmers use them around here."

"Okay. But *why* would he be on a quad bike? Dressed for business? And where is it now?"

Adam shrugged. "The best guess we have is that he was getting a lift with someone. It wasn't Tait because he was still in town, with witnesses. Nor was it Chloe. And perhaps, he fell from the back. That's what we're pursuing right now. We'll talk to everyone locally who might have had access to a quad."

"It sounds bizarre," I said.

He lowered his voice even further, and we all leaned in closer. "It gets more bizarre," he said. "This is the bit you need to keep to yourselves. I raised it with my bosses, but apparently I'm overthinking it. But you know, I didn't see any tracks there. Nothing in the snow. No tyres, no tracks, and no footprints. I was the first person on the scene."

"Who called you?"

"He did. He called 999 on his phone. He was lucky to get a signal. I was despatched, and the mountain rescue were mobilised too, but as they are volunteers and I was already on shift, I got there first. He had lost consciousness by the time I found him. The snow was falling but I could clearly see there was no sign of any tyre tracks at all."

"Did you take photographs? As evidence?"

He winced. "No. My priority was keeping him alive. Which failed, in the end." He shuddered. "So that's where we are at. I am supposed to be following a line of enquiry which I don't believe is right. There is something odd about it all. I am sure there will be a clear explanation, but…"

"Basically, you think someone killed him," I said.

His eyebrows shot up. "No. No! Not at all. I only mean that we don't really know *how* he died, and that concerns me. Don't jump to conclusions. Murders are very, very rare. Llanfair has had its fill, statistically." He stood up abruptly. "I have probably said too much. Look, don't get involved. Thanks for listening, and I am glad you got home safe." He moved to the door. "And look, the weather is forecast to remain pretty bad. Maybe even get worse. Stay inside. Have you got everything you need?"

"We're fine," Dilys said. "There's about half a cow in the freezer."

"Mmm. Nice," he said. "Right. I'll be off." I met his eyes, and he smiled, a little private secret smile just for me. I felt myself blush slightly.

"Stay safe yourself," I told him.

Then he let himself out, and Maddie nearly burst with excitement.

"We've got a crime to solve!"

Four

I was inclined to agree. "Right," I said. "Let's get official. Maybe I should start drinking coffee. That's what detectives do, isn't it? And get a long coat to wear. Should I smoke a cigar? First of all, though, do we *really* believe there was no foul play?"

"Hell no!" said Maddie.

"Hell to the no," Dilys said in a passable American accent, and we both stopped to stare at her for a moment.

"Well, coffee, then?" she said, meekly, getting to her feet.

"Thanks."

She went to the range to boil up the kettle. Maddie leaned her elbows on the table. "Tell me everything you know about David Hudson."

"I don't know any more than you, actually. He turned up last month with Chloe. She'd been working in London, I think. Might have been Cardiff. She left Llanfair years ago. She's one of the millions of people I know without really knowing. She comes back from time to time to visit her folks on their farm. And he's a horrible man. You know, I'm still angry about how he spoke to Aunt Dilys."

Maddie narrowed her eyes, and whispered to me, "Yeah, so about that. Can we be entirely sure that Dilys didn't, you know, kinda curse him a bit?"

"A bit? He's actually dead."

"Yeah. So could it have gone wrong, that curse? She did just predict his death in her tea leaves and all."

We both looked up at Dilys.

She was staring at us. "I am not deaf. I sometimes wish I was. Oh, the hurtful things that I hear…"

"Okay, then," I said. "*Did* you curse him?"

"No, I didn't. I should have. It's too late now. What a bother."

"Well, I am sure you'll catch up with him soon in the afterlife," I said.

Maddie drew in a sharp breath. She'd lived with us for over a month now, but still our harsh conversations could shock her. Dilys grated out a laugh, and said, "There's my fight with Mabel, remember? I'm going nowhere. Not yet. Can't you get hold of his shade?"

Maddie was staring hard at me. I had to grudgingly say, "Sorry, Aunt Dilys. And no, I can't. Well, I shouldn't. Especially not so that you can curse him. I mean, the guy is dead now. Seems unfair to make things any worse for him." And then we continued our analysis of the events.

Maddie tapped the table with her finger as she went over each point in turn. I noticed she had painted her nails bright red. She was using more make-up lately and I filed that point aside. Was that the Tylwyth Teg at work? She complained endlessly about the lack of decent hair products for her multi-racial hair type in our local shops. She'd taken to ordering large bottles of things that smelled like coconut off the internet.

"So, here is what we know," Maddie said, tapping. "David Hudson was found injured on the hills. He called for help but didn't regain consciousness before he died."

"Wait, we don't know that," I said.

"We can assume so, because otherwise he'd have told someone what happened," she said.

"Fair point. Go on."

"Right, so his injuries were really bad and suggested a fall from height or at speed. The police say it was likely to have been a vehicle of some kind."

"Yes, but…"

"Exactly, *but*. But there were no signs of any tracks at the scene. However, snow was falling pretty quickly. Could they have been covered up? Could Adam have been mistaken? Did he look far enough from the body? He admits he was concentrating on seeing to the injured man."

"I believe Adam," I said. "He can't turn his policeman-sense off. If he saw no tracks, there *were* no tracks."

"And Hudson was not dressed for walking, and we saw him a little over an hour previously, in his office." Maddie took a cup of coffee from Dilys, who sat herself down at the table with us. I sipped at mine. It was blisteringly hot and smelled bitter. I didn't like it. I was slightly surprised Maddie hadn't told me to start drinking liquidised grass and kale and stuff. Apparently coffee was exempt from "clean eating" as it was a "necessary food group."

"He has got to have been deliberately hurt," Maddie said. "It's all too strange."

"Murdered," I said. "He's dead, remember? Even if they didn't intend to kill him, he's dead now, so it is murder. Or manslaughter at the very least."

"So who would have wanted to kill him?" Maddie suddenly sucked in her cheeks. "Ooh, Bron, you did have a very public argument with him! That would make you a suspect."

"I am not!" I felt a little ill. If I were a police officer looking for a potential murderer, of course I'd ask people who'd recently argued with the victim. "Anyway, I wasn't the only one there. That would make you and Dilys suspects, too."

"Well, we are all innocent. The next really obvious one is Chloe, of course," Maddie pointed out. "She has to be top of the list."

I tried to drink the coffee but it was like licking a dry sponge. I put the unfinished cup on the table. "Definitely. Right! So let's go talk to her."

Maddie jumped to her feet when I did. "Where? What? When? How? This is exciting!"

I remembered the Reverend Horatio counselling me, some time ago, to be careful and mindful of sticking my nose into other people's business. Then I told myself that his advice wasn't relevant right now – if I was a suspect (which I wasn't) in a murder (which wasn't confirmed) then I totally needed to find out more facts for myself, right?

We got into our big coats, layered up with scarves and hats

and gloves and buffs and boots and socks and those little heated hand-warmer things that you shake to make hot, and sallied forth on our mission, out into the snow and cold of Llanfair.

***

The first thing we noted was that the business premises where we'd seen them before was all closed up. That, of course, was to be expected. There was no handy note on the door, unfortunately. I think I was hoping for "Due to the unforeseen murder of David Hudson by [someone], we will be closed until next Monday" or something. Sadly, that was not the case. There were no signs or notices or useful confessions.

"Right," said Maddie. "So where does Chloe live?"

"I don't know if she came back here to live with her family on the farm, or whether she got a place in town," I said. "The farm is a bit of a trek out from here, to be honest, especially in this weather."

"Billy."

"Billy?"

"Billy."

"Ah!" I said. "Yes, you're right. Billy will know."

So off we pottered, through the town centre, to Caffi Cwtch, the usual hang-out for our local down-and-nearly-out, Billy. Sometimes he had a few days of work doing labouring or general odd jobs for people, but most of the time, he sat in the café and endured Alston's spite.

Although, for all of Alston's muttered invectives against

"jobless wasters", I had never ever seen Billy have to pay for his drinks.

We struck gold. Today, the snow had clearly put people off from venturing into town, and the café was empty except for the one person that we wanted to see. We waved cheerily at Billy as we went up to the counter, made the minimum of polite small talk with the scowling Alston and then joined Billy on his table.

"He's got a three-for-two offer on sausage rolls," I lied rather too obviously as I pushed one across the table to Billy. "So you might as well have the spare one. Maddie won't let me eat two in one day."

"I don't think we ought to be eating even one," Maddie said as she prodded the pastry-cased pork meat with one long finger. She hadn't acquired a taste for all our British delicacies yet. "You never did explain what was really in one of these. 'Pork products and derivatives' could mean anything … but nothing good. Ugh, I guess we need the lard, given the weather."

"Exactly. So, Billy, what's new with you?"

"Not much. Got me some work, like, from the vicar, bless him, for Easter and that. He's a good man in spite of the church stuff. Heard that the snow is set to last for a week, they reckon. Oh, and that nugget Hudson went and smacked his head and carked it out on the tops, didn't he! Splat! Ha ha!"

Maddie briefly rested her head on her forearms. "Bron, you are gonna have to translate that for me, please. My mom is from here but she never, ever speaks like that."

Maddie's mother had moved from Wales when she was a teenager, and by now she had spent longer in America than anywhere else. She probably even sounded Californian.

Billy laughed and switched to Welsh for a few sentences, just to annoy her even more. Like I said before, my Welsh was pretty basic, but I understood that he was just repeating what he'd already told me in English.

"Ok, so Billy is working for the vicar and the snow is going to stay–"

"Okay, yeah, so I got that. What was the thing about the nuggets?" she asked.

"He just means that Hudson isn't well-liked," I said. "But he didn't cark it out on the hills, Billy. He died in hospital later on."

"But what was he doing up there?" Billy asked.

"That's what we want to know. Do you know anything about him, or his girlfriend?"

"I know Chloe. I've lived here all my life, isn't it? Chloe's from that farm up the other side of the valley, like."

"And is that where she lives now?"

"I'm not a stalker or anything."

"Do you want a top-up of tea?" I asked him sweetly.

"Uh, yeah, go on then. All right. So I think she lives in a house down Mill Row."

"Any chance you know the number?"

"That would be stalkerish," Billy said. "No, I don't."

I went up and got him a fresh cup of tea. We said our goodbyes, and headed for the line of terraced housing known as Mill Row.

***

The sky was darkening with the threat of a fresh dumping of snow to come. Cars drove past us with their lights on, such was the gloom. And this worked to our advantage, because many of the houses along Mill Row were lighting up from within.

We prowled along, glancing around as surreptitiously as we could, while trying not to look suspicious. We played at guessing which house might belong to Chloe – the one with the lacy net curtains? The one with the utilitarian vertical blinds, like an office? The one with the battered Land Rover outside, the four-wheel-drive vehicle apparently held together by tape and orange baler twine?

That made us stop. "She's in there!" Maddie gasped in my ear and she grabbed my arm to drag me to my knees. Together we huddled behind a parked car on the opposite side of the street.

"Who else did you see? Which house was it?" I asked.

"It was the window of the house behind that big green car," she said. "She was in there with some older couple. Maybe her parents? The woman looked a bit like her."

"Did she look upset? Or, I dunno, a bit … gloaty?"

"She didn't look murdery, no. She wasn't leaping about with a bloodied knife in her hand, cackling like Lady Macbeth. She looked blank, really. I suppose that's normal?"

I tried to peer around the car. Eyes, I realised, were in the wrong place for spying on other people. We needed to evolve eyes on stalks. I tried to angle my head so that less of my forehead would show.

40

"Are you all right?" Maddie asked. "Have you strained a muscle?"

"Not yet. Ugh, I can't see anything. Oh! Ahh, get down!"

"I'm already down, you dumbass!"

We hunkered down even further. I heard a door close and a masculine cough. I whispered to Maddie, "Someone was coming out of their house. I didn't see who."

Then there was the heavy slam of a car door. It opened again, and slammed again. Popped open, and slammed. This went on for about twenty seconds before the door stayed shut. Obviously it was an old vehicle with some mechanical issues – it had to be the ratty looking Land Rover. It could belong to her parents, I thought, as it was a typical farm vehicle.

The engine started up. It did not sound healthy. Some cars purr, some growl, but this one was hacking up a hairball. I shuffled sideways and peered around the side of the car, my fingers lightly touching the cold metal. "It's Edmund Tait!" I exclaimed, slightly louder than I intended to. Maddie shot to my side and popped her head up.

"So it is! There he goes. Well, he's a family friend, right? And we saw him before."

"He is, though I don't understand why someone like Chloe – educated, travelled, rising in the world – would remain friends with a scruffy farm worker like Tait."

"Oh, man, you are such a snob," Maddie said. "Maybe, you know, they are both actually decent people who can have a friendship without some weird-ass class system getting in the way and all?"

"Like you don't have the same in America," I said. "Except yours is based on money and ours is … money, and accent, and family, and what word you use for a toilet. Hush, now. Look, there he goes." I took the chance to glance at the window of the house. Chloe was standing there, looking out, a forlorn and lost expression on her face. Someone came up behind her, and drew her back into the room.

"Hey, so I've had an idea," Maddie said. We remained on our knees behind the parked car. "What if, right, Chloe and Tait were seeing one another? You know, like, having an affair? And what if, right, Tait is the killer? He's done away with his rival, Hudson?"

"It's a thought," I said. "And I think it's logical. But we really, really need to find out *how* he died. Remember what Adam said. That's the mystery."

"Get back!" Maddie hissed suddenly and grabbed my elbow. I was crouching rather precariously and I lost my balance. I ended up doing one of those slow-tumbles-of-inevitability, rocking back onto my bottom with my heels up in the air.

"What the?"

"There's a car going past … oh, a car stopping … quick, get up, let's run for it…"

I scrabbled up, and immediately ducked back down again. But it was too late. I had seen the police car, and the officer in the car had seen me. He rolled the window down and called out.

"Bron, Maddie, stand up, the pair of you."

It was Adam. Sheepishly, we rose to our feet. "Hi, Adam. I just dropped an earring and we were looking for it," I said.

He leaned his arm on the window. "You don't have your ears pierced."

I was briefly flattered that he had noticed. "It was one of those clip-on ones?"

He shook his head. "Then you've lost both of them. And you've never worn them before. And you're obviously lying. Come on, get in." He got out of the car and opened up the rear door. "I'll take you both home."

"We're not going home!"

"You are," he said, in a firm voice, "because someone called the police station to tell us about two women behaving very suspiciously. So get in, and tell me what you're up to. Then I can decide whether to arrest you or just laugh at you."

Reluctantly, we slid into the panda car. He slammed the doors and I knew we were trapped; these things didn't open from the inside.

"Bron, will you damp down your … effects … as much as you can, please?" he asked.

For a childish moment I wanted to unleash the full force of my energy-curse, and totally mess up all the tech that was lighting up the dashboard of the car. But I didn't. I sighed and drew a circle around myself. "I'll do my best," I muttered, "but there's so many gadgets and gizmos in here that I can't guarantee I won't blow something up or fry a circuit or something."

"We won't be long. You concentrate on not destroying my car, and Maddie, you can tell me what you're up to. It's not a coincidence that you were outside Chloe Davies's house, is it?"

"Oh, tell him, Maddie," I said, and retreated into my safe

43

bubble as the car set off and we trundled down the road.

"There's nothing to tell," she said, and I could detect a light sweetness in her voice that suggested she was using her glamour to weave a little spell over her words. "We talked about the unfortunate death of David Hudson after you left, and we were worried about Chloe, of course, so we came out and happened to wander past. Bron thought she might be able to assist. As a healer, you know? But then we saw that her family was with her, so we moved on."

"And the earring? And the hiding? And the fact that someone rang us up to say that two women were either casing a house for a burglary or planning to steal a car?"

"Oh, that's just nonsense," Maddie said. "When we saw she wasn't alone, we decided that we didn't want to be seen because, of course, that would look so horrible and intrusive."

Adam huffed but Maddie's flippant tone was obviously working on him, because he didn't challenge us any further. He did say, as he pulled up outside our house, "If you *must* think about things, then be logical. Don't just wander around, relying on intuition."

"Of course. But we'll leave the real detectoring to you!" Maddie trilled.

Adam got out and released us from the car. "I mean it," he cautioned. "I don't want to get any more calls about you two. And remember, also – the only question is *how he died*. Okay?"

Maddie waved and I shrugged, and we plodded back into the house.

***

I went into the kitchen first, and I stepped quietly, because some of the injured animals that I passed in the utility room were sleeping. The hedgehog had been released almost immediately, but there remained a mix of domestic and wild animals under my care.

Dilys was still in the kitchen with her back to me, and she jumped. She was wearing a black knitted shawl and I thought that I saw her shove something underneath it. It could have been a book, a large hardback of some description, judging from the angular lump that it made below the fabric.

"Oh! I didn't hear you come in, *cariad*," she said. Her eyes flicked past me to where Maddie was following behind.

"Sorry. I didn't mean to startle you. Are you okay?" I meant it; she looked strained, and tired. I was conscious of her age, and that all our banter might have been masking a very real concern that we all had: my great aunt would not last forever, in spite of her stubborn determination to do exactly that.

"Of course I am okay!" she snapped back, just like her usual self. "No thanks to you creeping up on a body to shock them into the middle of next week, though. It's a wonder I haven't had seven heart attacks and a stroke."

"I *said* I was sorry," I retorted, immediately becoming a stupid child once more. Funny how you're an adult most of the time, but when you are interacting with someone who has always been in a parental position over you, you revert to how you used to be. Or maybe it's just me, and I need to do some growing up.

Whatevs.

Maddie breezed past me, in full-on peacekeeper mode once more. "So, we've just been to see Chloe!" she announced.

"We didn't, really. I wouldn't count it as seeing. More like, spying," I said.

"Yes, yes, that too."

Dilys cocked her head to one side. "Really? How is she doing? Is she coping?"

"She looked sad. But that's understandable, right?" Maddie said.

"She does have a thread of sadness running through her," Dilys said. "She always has had."

"How well do you know her?" Maddie asked.

Dilys paused. I felt acres of meaning in that pause. "Aunt?" I pressed. "There is something you're not telling us."

"I have to respect confidentiality," she said at last.

"What do you mean?" I blurted out. "Confidentiality? Do you mean she's actually consulted you?"

"Nearly half the folk in this town have spoken to me at some point," Dilys said.

"Before she left for London or wherever … or since she came back with Hudson?"

Dilys frowned. "Well, then. It was London, you know. She came to see me a fortnight ago."

"Two weeks?" Maddie whispered to me. "That right?"

"No, two sennights," I hissed back. "Okay yes, two weeks."

"She just wanted to see her future, just the same as anyone does," Dilys went on. "But I didn't see much. Sometimes, when someone is in such a state of uncertainty and flux, it's actually impossible to see anything clearly."

"But surely, if you can see the future, you can still see what is going to happen?" Maddie said.

"The web of wyrd is not woven like that," Dilys said. "I can see the patterns in the cloth, and predict the likely pattern yet to come; but she was at such a crossroads that the Fates had not yet decided what was to become of her. Or, if they had, they were not inclined to share their knowledge with me this time. So it goes."

I think we all understood the vagaries of our dealings with the mystical side of life. Especially Maddie, now that she was working more closely with the fickle Faerie themselves. We accepted Dilys's explanation.

"Did she talk about her relationship with David Hudson?" I asked.

Dilys turned away from me, still clutching the object under her shawl. "It was stormy, but you could see that yourself. He wasn't right for her, but I could not tell her that. She had to see it for herself. And she suspected that, anyway. Right, you two, I need to get on. And you have some salve to make up for Mr Edwards. He came by to collect it, but I couldn't see that it was ready yet. Your shelves are looking empty, Bron."

I cursed to myself. I'd let myself get distracted and yes, I was behind on my herbal remedies. "I'll get onto it," I said. "But listen, Aunt, why didn't you mention all this before? The stuff with Chloe?"

"I haven't told you anything new, so it wasn't relevant," she snapped. Still hiding the object, she bustled her way out of the kitchen and into the hallway.

"What was she hiding, do you think?" I said to Maddie, meaning the thing under her shawl.

But Maddie thought I meant something else. "She just wants to protect you," she said.

I stared at her.

"I'm sorry," Maddie said. "Don't worry about it." And she dashed off the way that Dilys had gone.

I was left alone in the kitchen, feeling quite confused.

Five

I got on with everyday stuff. What else was there to do? Don't they say that before Enlightenment, you chop wood and carry water. And after Enlightenment, you … still chop wood and carry water. My animals needed tending to, my spring garden needed attention, and I had herbal cures to make up and deliver.

We were in that part of the year we call The Hungry Gap. Most animals have exhausted their food stores by this time, and back in the days before supermarkets and all-year-round produce, so had humans. But new growth was not yet here, and the hedgerows would be bare of food. All around, everything was in the state of Just-About-To-Grow – but there was nothing to eat.

I scattered bird seed under the bushes for the ground-feeders, and up on the high ledges I'd attached to walls and fences, and from the dangling platforms that were supposed to deter squirrels. I suspected our squirrels – sadly the ubiquitous greys which have overrun the red population all across Britain – to be ninja types, capable of leaping great distances in their pursuit of food. Still, I topped up the food and hoped the birds would be able to grab some before they were raided by the furry flying rats.

I tried not to think about the mysterious death of David Hudson. Not that I was avoiding the issue – no, I just find my brain works better if I leave it alone to chunter away under the surface. I let my subconscious do the work. This does mean, however, that sometimes I don't know what I actually know, and I take myself by surprise when I speak.

That's my excuse for my tactless outbursts, anyway.

When I wandered back into the kitchen, my hands and face frozen solid, I encountered Great Aunt Dilys again. She was sitting down at the table and chopping vegetables.

"Cawl tonight?" I asked, spying a neck of lamb in a bowl by the growing pile of leeks, parsnips and swede.

"Yes, I think we all need something warming. There's more cold weather on the way."

"Aunt, can I ask you something?" I went to the range and leaned my hands against the brass rail that ran along the front of it. It was a solid-fuel cooking and heating appliance that was always on. It would soon thaw me out. "Can you use your gift to seek out what happened to David Hudson, up on the hill, when he fell?"

"You already know the answer to that," Dilys said, scraping a carrot.

"Yes, I know you have always said that your gift only works with people directly," I said. "But then you saw 'death' in the tea leaves, so you must be able to … uh, I don't know. Branch out a little?"

"I see the future, not the past," she reminded me. "And it

50

is true, I do only work with people."

"But–"

She picked up a large knife and began to hack at the carrot. She didn't watch what she was doing. Instead, she fixed me with her glare. "Which means, when I saw that word – death – in the leaves, that the message was directly connected with someone in this house."

In spite of the furnace to my back, I went ice-cold right down my spine.

***

Maddie had disappeared that afternoon and I caught up with my work. She hadn't gone to work, as far as I knew. I assumed, therefore, she was working on her gift. When she came back inside, her eyes were watering and her skin was cold. She'd been outside, and when she spoke, her voice was hoarse.

She shook her head when I asked what she'd been doing, and ran upstairs to get a bath.

At our evening meal that night – which we called tea, being Welsh, and she called dinner, being contrary – our conversation turned once more to the death, and it made me resolve to do more to find out what had happened.

I decided that later that night, I would go hedge riding.

It was a comment from Dilys that forced me to make up my mind, in the end. After all, strolling the boundaries of the worlds is not something anyone does lightly and without cause. I began to see, however, that I did, indeed, have a compelling reason.

"Of course," Dilys said, as we were mulling over the friendship between Edmund Tait and Chloe Davies, "the Taits and the Davieses go way back."

I wanted to fling my cutlery down and have a dramatic hissy fit. I reminded myself that I was an adult and we had to now pretend to be calm, at least on the outside. I sighed and said, "Excuse me? Aunt? Another revelation?"

"It's hardly a revelation when it's common knowledge."

"*I* did not know. What do you mean, they go way back?"

"Well, it's two old farming families, isn't it? They've been on opposite sides of the valley for generations."

"Most of the farms around here have been around for generations. What's so special about the relationship between those two?"

"I am probably reading too much into it," Dilys said, infuriating me. "Could you pass me more bread, *bach*?"

I shoved the plate across the table. "Tait and Chloe are around the same age," I said. "I suppose they will have gone to school together."

"Wouldn't they have been at the same school as you?" Maddie asked.

"I remember Chloe. She was two years above me, and she was fierce on the hockey team. I don't remember Tait. All the older boys were just one smelly indistinguishable lump. Except for Bobby, of course…"

"Bobby who?" Maddie pressed, her eyes lighting up.

"I can't even remember his last name. It doesn't matter."

Dilys cackled. "Her first crush! You wrote his name over and over in your exercise book."

"I did not!"

"You did," she said, "Because I kept it and I have it hidden away."

"Why?"

"Why do you think? I might need to embarrass you in the future. I will bring it out when the time is right. When it can cause maximum shame."

"Well, why change the habit of a lifetime," I said. But my heart wasn't in the banter. I was thinking about farms, and connections to the land, and history, and ancestors, and what it could mean for Edmund Tait and Chloe Davies.

But – still, however guilty the pair of them now looked to me – how? HOW had they done it?

***

Harkin was at my feet before I'd even been aware that I'd called him to me. He pressed against my ankles, reassuring me.

I felt nervous.

But then, I always felt a little nervous. I had vowed to myself that the moment I didn't feel afraid of leaving my body and riding on the corpse roads, the Ways Between The Worlds, the narrow place and the hedges of consciousness: that moment, I would have to stop. Fear kept me alert to the dangers. Fear would keep my mind sharp and save me.

I have a lot of sympathy with those who rail against the use of magic, you know. It is a powerful thing and like anything powerful, there's danger there. Horatio, the local vicar, knew this and kept an eye on me from afar. Complacency will, at the very least, send you mad. If you're lucky. If you're unlucky? Let's not go there. I'd say "you can imagine" but you really, really can't, and trust me – that is a good thing.

I took a bath and emptied my mind. I drank some water flavoured with lemon, and Harkin waited patiently outside on the landing until I emerged wearing good, stout outdoor clothing.

What, no robes? Or even better, "skyclad?" Oh, that daft myth.

Okay, so yeah I did pick up my nice big cloak from the utility room on my way outside. But if magic is powerful enough to travel through time and space, it can definitely get through a pair of flannel-lined walking trousers and sturdy boots. The cloak was warm, roomy and only used for hedge riding, so I guess it did have some mystical significance for me. It might just have been the state of mind it triggered, but that was enough.

I spent a little while standing in the garden. There was a waning moon, which wasn't my favoured time to travel. It was good for meeting the spirits of the dead, but it brought additional dangers. It certainly wasn't a positive time of growth and expansion, like the waxing moon.

As for the nights where there was no moon at all, those nights were something else and I had only travelled on a night like that once, towards the beginning of my apprenticeship to the Other Worlds, and it wasn't something I'd choose to do again any time soon.

The moon lit the snowy garden up like it was the middle of the afternoon. I could hear a bird singing, confused by the light. The sky was pocked by ragged fluffy grey clouds riding high in the sky where I could see the winds were stronger. They scudded over the moon from time to time.

I felt a push from behind like a hand in the small of my back. There was, of course, no one there. Harkin mewed, and I knew that it was time.

I crawled into my willow cave. Even in winter, with the flexible withies bare and stark, it was a snug little place. I sat on a heap of old, brown leaves and moss, and crossed my legs. I had everything I needed within arm's reach, and soon I had a small fire blazing between me in the cave, and the rest of the garden outside.

I looked at the flame.

And after a while, the flame began to look back at me.

I remained where I was, Harkin curled in my lap, and at the same time I began to descend a set of steps in blackness until I stood on a shore of silver sand and let the rising dark water inch its way up my legs, my body and my neck until I was sinking down. Then I kicked out my feet and rose, hurtling upwards until I burst out into the night air and found myself in flight, suspended above our house and garden.

I could just see the red glow of the fire. I had never gone down to see myself from the outside. I didn't like to think about it. Mirrors are bad enough. I turned around and rose up on a thermal.

I had an aim. I had to: people who wander without purpose

out here are brave, or foolish, and I suppose – I hope – that I am neither. I wanted to seek out David Hudson's shade or spirit, if it was still around, and see if I could ask it what had happened.

It's never as easy as that sounds, unfortunately.

I flew with black wings over the town. I am not a shapeshifter. I leave that to the likes of Rachel Harris, a woman I encountered with the previous mysterious death in our town. No, I was myself, but I was partnered by – or allowed to ride with – Her, my Raven Mistress. She was not my familiar, though the popular books with shiny curly letters on the black and purple covers will have you think that She was. I myself would not dare to downgrade Her so.

We flew, two spirits in one, heading through the bitterly cold air to the place where Hudson had died.

Ghosts are funny things. It's not like a carbon copy of the living person hangs around, with their full consciousness and memory. If they do, well, that must be rare because I've never met them. Instead, snippets can linger. Sometimes, it's almost like the whole person, and that's a problem because it means something is tying them to the earthly plane; part of my job, my second, hidden, secret job, is to release these people, through ritual and path-working.

Usually the unfinished business tying the spirit down was relatively mundane. Murder, however, was sure to be another reason, and I wondered what it would mean if I saw a lot of David Hudson's spirit remaining. Perhaps it would suggest foul play.

I reached the hillside where he'd fallen, and turned a wide

circle as I studied what I could see below me, using human and bird senses both.

There was definitely something down there.

Something otherwordly.

Success, I thought, and began a spiralling descent, my speed increasing with each banking turn.

The dark shape on the white snow was hunched over, or at least, that was how it looked from above. But as I wheeled around it, it seemed to unfold, and I realised with a jolt that this was no human shape.

Frantically I flapped my wings, desperate to gain height before it became aware of me. I had no idea what I was looking at, and I didn't want to encounter it before I was sure of what I was facing.

There was a bad, bad feeling about the thing down there.

The air around me shifted, fighting me, forcing me down. I dragged air into my lungs and clawed my way upwards, pressing against the shadow that was reaching out to me.

It knew I was here.

There was a buzzing in my head as I called on all my strength and all that She could lend to me. The buzzing grew louder, threatening to break my essential concentration.

At last I broke free, my shoulders straining, my lungs bursting, and suddenly I was atop a warm air current and flying unencumbered.

Yet, curiously, the buzzing in my head remained with me all the way back to my willow cave.

And as I listened to it, it changed pitch. It formed words.

The buzzing became a song. I caught only fragments of words, but they danced relentlessly in my head, a malevolent earworm.

"…the hooves that touch no soil, no soil …"

"…fleet … tear your soul, your soul …"

"…no soil, no soil …"

"…no soul."

SIX

I returned to myself, and thanked all the spirits and the genii loci and, of course, Her, for their protection and guidance. I remained in the willow cave as the flames burned down. I fed them a little of my hair and my spit and they gave a quick flare of green in acknowledgment, and then the fire was gone, and Harkin was uncurling and purring and licking my hands, urging me to get inside and eat something so as to ground myself.

As I went across the paving slabs outside the backdoor, my foot hit a metal plate with a clang, and spun it into the blackness.

I stumbled into the kitchen, my mind still a blur, the buzzing song roaring in my head. Dilys had waited up for me – Maddie was working at Sian's shop the next day, so she had gone to bed – and there was a plate of easy-to-eat food ready on the table. I slid into a chair and picked at the cheese and crackers while Dilys made up a hot toddy.

She must have seen from my face that I wasn't ready to talk yet. Suddenly the plate was empty. I supposed I must have eaten it all, and Dilys led me quietly up to bed.

The next day, I missed Maddie before she went off to the shop. I went out to the back step where we had a rough patio area – if twelve cracked grey paving slabs count as a "patio" – and saw that she had picked up the bowl from where I had kicked it the previous night.

I smiled. She was taking her studies of the Tylwyth Teg very seriously. She did a lot of reading of folklore, and Sian was helping her with the modern interpretations of the dangerous elemental forces, and now she was beginning to make her own connections with them. I didn't like it, but I knew she had to. It was her path. Her thread in the web of wyrd, if you like. I reminded myself that she could trust them to look after her.

One of the aspects that Maddie was exploring was the feeding of the Faerie, and she had taken up the old country custom of leaving out a little milk and bread for them. It was a tradition that the Fair Folk were thanked for their work around the house.

There were two problems with that.

The first was that, as far as I could see, they did nothing in the house. In the old stories they clean grates and so on, and if you ignore them, they spoil the milk. Our house has always been a Faerie-free place, and the sprites do us neither harm nor good. They had no place here.

And the second problem – born of the first, that we had no Faerie in the house – was that the plate or bowl she put out only attracted unwelcome visitors of a very non-mystical form, namely, the common rat. I didn't have the heart to tell her, but nor did I want to risk the lives of the ill and injured animals in the utility room. It was fairly rat-proof but not immune, and I had noticed Harkin had become tired. He was staying up all night to guard the injured creatures.

So I had begun to remove the bread and milk from the bowl after she had gone to bed, and leave the platter empty, so that when she revisited it in the morning, she believed the Faerie Folk had taken her gift.

I should have spoken to her about it right away, when she first did it.

I would probably have to tell her at some point. I went back inside and wondered how, and knew that I'd probably let it go on too long already.

But she was my cousin and I thought – when I started the well-meaning deception – that it would be a way of supporting her. I had spent a long time trying to secretly make the oils she wanted for her hair, but by the time I'd perfected it, she'd already ordered a dozen bottles, and my surprise was no longer needed. Every time I was about to speak to her, she was engulfed in what I thought was a new disappointment – the lack of internet so she couldn't skype home, for example.

There had never been a good time to tell her to stop putting food out. I had taken it up on a spur of the moment impulse.

And now it was probably too late. I was stuck on this course and probably doomed to pick up half-rotten food from the patio for ever more.

I shook it from my mind. It was hardly important right now.

I did some gardening and sowed some seeds, wrapping plastic bags over the pots and putting them on the windowsill in a warm spot, but the pruning would have to wait as everything outside was too snowy and frosty.

Maddie returned at midday, with the rest of the day at her leisure. It was snowing again, very lightly. We fried up some leftover mashed potato and vegetables with eggs and bacon, and while we ate our dinner, she asked me a question. Luckily it wasn't about the Faeries taking the bread and milk every night.

"Hey, so you never told me about the stone circle! Where is it?"

"We don't have any stone circles. Not locally, anyway. I can't think where the nearest one might be."

"Sure you do. Someone was asking me about it, but obviously I didn't know. I was going to ask Sian but she was out and when she came back to take over from me, it was pretty busy."

"Nah, they must be mistaken," I said. "I mean, I don't think I could have missed a great heap of stones around the place. Someone's messing with you."

There was a brief rat-a-tat at the back door, and Adam stuck his head in.

"Hey there, how's it going?" he said.

"Come in, grab a pew, have a brew," I said, waving at him in delight.

Maddie grinned at me.

I raised one eyebrow.

She mouthed, "you owe me" and got to her feet, saying,

"Oh, do excuse me, Adam. I think I heard Dilys calling."

"She's subtle," Adam said as he came into the kitchen and Maddie left by the other door. "But I passed your aunt in town. She was helping Jemima patch up some man in overalls. Might have been the meter reader. I think her parrot's been on the rampage again."

He waved me back to my seat, and helped himself to a cup of tea from the half-stewed pot on the table.

"You on duty?" I asked.

"Just finished," he said. "I've done a half-shift to cover for Pol who had to go to the opticians or something."

"So what's the word on the case?"

"That's why I am here," he said, and he looked glum. "There is no case. Or, well, it's case closed, soon. They are going to just file it away and not look for anyone else in connection with it."

"How can they do that? A man is dead!"

"But there isn't any evidence to suggest anything untoward. There will be an inquest. I don't know whether they will record a death by misadventure, by accident or just an open verdict, but regardless of the final wording, we won't be looking into it any further."

"And you disagree, don't you?"

"I do," he said. "What do you think? Have your – senses – picked anything up?" Adam looked a little uncomfortable. He knew of all my gifts, and the curse, but he didn't fully understand them.

Well, let's be honest, neither did I.

I told him, briefly and lightly, about my adventure the

previous night. I concluded with, "There was something otherworldly down there, Adam, I am sure of it."

"But what? And anyway, it could be totally unconnected with Hudson's death."

"It could," I admitted. "There are things that feed on places where bad things happened. It could just be some kind of astral scavenger. And yet, I agree with you. This death was suspicious. Surely Chloe is the main suspect? And her friend, Edmund Tait?"

"And most of the other people he ever encountered in his life," Adam pointed out. He rubbed at his face. "He was not well liked. But I can't do anything more about it. And I can't ask you to look into it, either."

"But…?"

"But I can ask you out on a date," he said, and grinned in a way that made my stomach flip a little.

We had tried doing the normal things like meals at restaurants. We'd soon discovered neither of us were any good at sitting in posh places and appreciating food we couldn't pronounce. "Where?" I said. "Skydiving, husky-running, scuba-diving?"

"High-ropes, I thought," he said. "There's a place about twenty miles away. Fancy it?"

"That's those things that are like high-level obstacle courses, all bridges and stuff between trees?"

"That's right. They do motocross, llama trekking, quad biking, all sorts of stuff, but the high-ropes looks best. I'll let you know when I get my shift pattern sorted. Any particular days bad for you?"

"No, I can be free anytime. Sounds great!" I said but I was already thinking of something else. His words had given me an idea.

***

Maddie was eager to try out my plan.

"We could use your glamour, I think," I said as we went out on foot, well dressed against the cold. Delicate snowflakes settled on our hats and noses. It was light, pretty, well-behaved snow, picture-postcard stuff.

"Sure," she assured me. "I want to be of use."

She meant, she didn't want to be the trusty sidekick. I gave her a brief one-armed hug.

"Gerroff," she said, laughing.

We decided we'd go up towards Blue Hill Farm. We passed through the edge of town, cooing over the snowmen – and snowwomen, and snowdogs, and a few snowblobs – that we saw in people's gardens. It seemed that the schools were still open, however, and we didn't see any kids indulging in snowball fights. That didn't stop Maddie, who threw four or five at me until I got annoyed and ordered her to stop.

"Mean," she said, shoving her hands into her jacket. "I know this snow won't last for long. Anyway, tell me about last night."

Her question came out of nowhere and I didn't feel ready to tell her, yet. Adam was different. Adam was non-magical and I downplayed the sheer other-ness of my journeying. But Maddie, though she was not a hedge rider, knew a little of what I faced. The song filled my head again, just those random repeated words.

No soul.

"It was odd," I said cautiously. We turned off the road and began to follow a farm track. Maddie jumped to the side so that she could walk in the fresh snow, and I copied her. It was fun to crunch through the white stuff, like a child again.

"How so? Hey, if you don't wanna talk about it, that's cool."

"Thanks. Yeah, no … well, I didn't learn anything useful. I did encounter something that felt *wrong* up where he died, but that was all. I need to let it linger in my head a little while. And now I have a song stuck in my head."

"What song?"

"I have no idea," I said. "Ah! Hello, Floss."

A black and white collie sheepdog came bounding out of the farmyard, so I knew either Gordon or Lynn would be around. Floss's excited yip brought a short, stocky woman to the door of a shed. She waved at us, and beckoned us over. We stepped into a warm, dark lambing shed. It was divided into pens, and filled with straw and the squeaky bleats of new lambs.

Lynn looked tired. Lambing could start in December in more temperate parts of the UK, but here on the hills, the lambing started properly after the worst of the winter weather had gone. Even so, this snow had caught people out. And some ewes would always give birth early. No doubt she was already working around the clock with her husband.

I introduced Maddie. Lynn's eyes flickered between us when I said she was my cousin; this was absolutely true. Our mothers were sisters. But Maddie's mother had left for America decades ago, married an African-American man, and settled in California. We looked alike if you studied our eyes, deep-set and green. But our skin tones and hair were very different. I was blonde, and rosy-cheeked, whereas she had deep brown hair that mostly curled but had its fair share of short kinky bits around her face that drove her mad.

Lynn, like all the inhabitants of Llanfair, didn't say a word to our faces about Maddie's ethnicity, in spite of the fact that the town was otherwise completely and monolithically white. I hadn't heard any gossip, either, which had surprised me. In truth I wasn't listening very hard for it, in case I heard something I needed to challenge, as I was not sure quite how to do that. Biting people's noses off was not going to be the answer.

"Are they all right?" Maddie was saying, leaning over the pen next to us and cooing at the rather-more-slimy-than-fluffy lambs.

"They will be," Lynn said, smiling at the twin lambs that were being licked and nuzzled by their mother. They were skinny, leggy and covered in goo, sprawled in the straw. "They'll be on their feet in no time." Lynn reached out and pulled a wide heat lamp down closer to them. "Now, what can I do for you girls?"

"Do you use quad bikes on the farm?" I asked.

She smiled. "Of course we do. You know, the police came around asking that, too. Why do you ask?"

"I have been trying to show my cousin around the area, and there are some amazing views to be had from some of the higher hills. We were wondering if we might borrow one? We'll pay for the fuel, of course."

Lynn knitted her brows together, though she kept smiling. "Well, er, I don't know, to be honest with you. It's a funny request, isn't it. Have you driven one before?"

I had never been able to drive in my life: I was always concentrating too hard on not blowing the engine up. It occurred to me that this might be a bad idea. I had assumed that quad bikes were simple things, and therefore easy for me to shield myself from. I suppose I thought they were like mechanical four-wheeled bicycles, not actual vehicles with electrics.

Yes. I am an idiot.

"Maddie, didn't you drive in America?" I said.

"Yeah, so I did Drivers' Ed, sure."

"Our agricultural quad bikes only have one seat, and you can't take them on the roads." Lynn shook her head. "It's not the best idea, especially right now with the snow on the hills. But perhaps–"

The air around us shimmered. I was all ready to back down and accept Lynn's refusal and my own stupidity, but Maddie had switched on her natural glamour. Now that she was exploring her link with the Tylwyth Teg more closely, she was able to harness that energy more effectively, day by day. Her study was paying off.

As for me, I still wanted to stay well away from the Fair Folk, the Faerie. They made me nervous with their beautiful fake faces and high pitched laughter. Maddie assured me that they weren't evil, but nor were they good. "Chaotic neutral" she said, but that meant nothing to me. They were like toddlers, but with powers beyond their morality.

Although Maddie was directing it at Lynn, even I couldn't fail to be affected by the edges of the power. Everything seemed brighter but hazier, colours vibrant but with soft and fuzzy edges, like photos that had been manipulated. I felt like I was sinking back into the soft green grass of a summer meadow.

Lynn was hit harder than I was. She smiled dreamily and swayed a little. "Oh, the quad bikes? They're easy enough if you can drive a manual car, even easier if you have ridden a motorbike."

Maddie's concentration broke a little.

Lynn was still influenced, however. "You shouldn't really take two people on one but the second person can cling on. Our kids always managed. Hey, if Floss here can do it, you can! I'll show you."

She led us out of the barn and across the yard to a long shed which was open on one side. It contained a vast array of machinery, and tucked to the back was a small, muddy, red four-wheeled vehicle.

"Are you sure about this?" I hissed at Maddie.

"How hard can it be?"

Lynn, still moving like an automaton, demonstrated how to turn it on. "It's one down, four up," she said, some mystifying code that I nodded at anyway. "Change gear with that pedal there. And off you go!"

She pottered away, humming, back to see to her lambs.

The quad bike thrummed away in neutral.

"Go on, then," I said to Maddie. "You started this."

"It was your idea."

"I don't think I thought it through properly."

"It's too late now."

"So, go on," I said to her. "You're the one that can drive."

"I learned in an automatic. What even are gears?"

"Get on," I told her. "But I'll walk alongside while you get used to it."

She sat on the scruffy seat, pulled at the clutch, pressed a pedal, and stalled it in a grunty flutter of smoke.

Silence descended.

With a set, grim mouth, she fired it up again, and half-closed her eyes as she pulled at levels, pressed at pedals, and felt for the change in engine note that would tell her she was getting it right. I stepped out of the way, and closed my circle down around myself, so as not to interfere with whatever scant electrics inhabited the vehicle.

It only took seven more false starts and juddering lurches before she was able to trundle it across the farm yard. Lynn popped her head out of the lambing shed once more. "Change gear! Change up!"

The engine was screaming now; Maddie managed to leap it up into second gear by some miracle, and by that point she was motoring with an unstoppable feeling of inevitability towards a gate. I found a burst of speed from nowhere, and got to the gate just in time to swing it open so she could lurch through. I closed it behind her, and set off at a jog as she drove at a random diagonal across a snowy field.

"Where are you heading?" I called, my feet sinking into the

snow.

"Just … out of sight of the farm," she said. "I'll wait the other side of that stand of trees. I need to find the next gear … wheee!"

With a grating sound, and a high-pitched whining, the quad bike jumped forward and churned up a great spray of snow and mud before disappearing around a small coppice.

We were supposed to be seeing how easy it was to fall from a quad bike by careful experiment, not by replicating David Hudson's unfortunate accident exactly.

With a sense of foreboding, I upped my pace.

Snow began to fall more heavily.

SEVEN

I rounded the copse of trees, out of breath and clutching at my side. So much for the miracles of healthy food. I half-expected to see a scene of devastation, with Maddie lying in the snow, the quad bike upturned and the obligatory flaming wheel rolling out of the wreckage.

Instead, I saw nothing more exciting than Maddie sitting atop the idling quad bike, smiling at me with a definite air of cocky triumph about her.

"Come on, then!" she said. "This is fun. Do you wanna climb on, or what?"

I was reluctant, but we'd come this far. "Yeah, okay. So now we need to check out that theory about him falling from a quad that someone else was driving." I discovered that although I could not sit anywhere, I was able to stand astride the seat behind Maddie, and cling on, my hands on her shoulders.

"Are you ready?" she said.

"I'm holding on, and I am shielding myself," I told her. "It should be enough. Go steady…"

The quad only stalled twice this time before she was able

to get it moving again. Snow got into our eyes. I gripped her tightly and shouted into her ear, "Do you know how fast this thing will go?"

"I'm not sure. Maybe thirty, forty miles an hour? That's just a guess. But anyway that would be on the road. We're doing fifteen right now."

"Really? Is that all? Feels like more!" I was only just able to hold on. We bounced from side to side. "Could you go faster?" I knew that we shouldn't. But we had to test things.

"Not easily on this terrain, no." She revved it up anyway, to my delight, and we picked up a little more speed, and it was enough to dislodge me. My stomach tightened and my arms flailed, and then I was in a heap in the freezing cold – but luckily soft – snow.

She made a circle and came to a halt, killing the engine. "You okay?"

I sat up. "Yes. Not only am I not dead, I am not injured at all."

She rubbed the snow from her eyebrows. She looked briefly disappointed. "Really?"

"Thanks for the concern."

"Yeah, you're welcome. So do we really think that Hudson could have fallen from a quad?"

"No. Not unless it was travelling at twice the speed we were going, and that would be impossible on the terrain that he was found on. And even then, falling into snow wouldn't do him much harm at all, I don't reckon."

Maddie looked up. "The sky looks a bit dark," she said.

"Guess we should head back."

I got to my feet and refused the offer of a lift as she started the engine. "That was enough for me. I'll walk," I told her, "and see you back at the farm."

***

Lynn looked confused when we handed her the keys, but Maddie smiled and prattled on and Lynn was steam-rolled by her twinkling onslaught. She was still in the lambing shed, and had been joined by her husband, who looked as tired as she was.

"We lost one just now," he said sadly.

"I should have been here," I said. "I could have helped."

"Some things can't be helped," he said. "It was not going to live long. But, thank you. You had best make tracks though; the storm is coming."

We took our leave and his words only hit me as we stepped out into the darkening air.

"The storm?" I said. "Wouldn't he say *a* storm? *The* storm makes it sound a bit significant. Portentous."

"It sure feels that way," Maddie said, and she pulled her scarf up around her chin. "But as long as we stick to the track, we'll be fine, right? Bad stuff only happens when you stray from the path. That's, like, the law. Every horror movie sticks to that law."

The wind came in gusts, attacking us sideways, and the sky was looking more like late evening. The snow swirled around and the air was freezing cold. We ploughed on, eager to get into the town where houses might afford us a little more shelter.

"Yeah," I said, blinking the snow from my vision. "We'll be fine. We can't get lost."

We kept a stone wall to our right hand side, and made painful progress along the farm track. Suddenly Maddie stopped and tried to look up.

"What is that?"

I could hear a screeching, almost braying sound, high up in the tearing black clouds. "It sounds a bit like geese," I said to her.

"Really? Do geese here fly in weather like this?"

"No, never," I said. "Nothing does." *Nothing … of this world*, I thought.

"But there is something up there," she said, half-shouting now as the roaring, shrieking noise grew louder. She clung to me, and I was grateful for the sudden human touch. I grabbed her in return and we tried to make out what was above us.

Invisible hands buffeted me. I had the impression of hooves, and howling, and laughter, too – a deep, male laughter.

I was filled with a strange sensation. There was no malevolence here, none at all! Just a joyous, unfettered lust for life – and hunting, and killing.

I shivered. That was *not* my normal state of mind.

But whatever was up there had a bloodlust and it was infectious. It felt like a rollercoaster screaming over us, pulled by braying hounds. A horn sounded.

Then it was gone, and I knew exactly what we had just encountered.

Still the wind tore around us, and Maddie pressed herself against me, trembling. This was the very opposite to her Faerie power. This was raw energy, honest, open, troubling, and direct. It was the thrill of the chase, and the delight in the victory.

It was dangerous but it was not evil.

"That," I whispered to her, "was the Wild Hunt. And we need to get home, right now."

EIGHT

I tried to explain the Wild Hunt to Maddie on the way home as we battled through the rising storm, but it turned out to be really difficult to put something like that into words. It had been a visceral knowledge that I'd always carried within me; but I realised I didn't know much about it, logically or intellectually. I felt frustrated because I'd always prided myself on my local knowledge. But maybe this was more about a deep understanding, rather than an outward word-bound logic.

As I stumbled through my explanation, I was left doubting myself.

"Oh," I ended up saying, "it's just an old wives' tale to explain the cries of the wild geese."

"But there were no geese," she said.

"I think it is something to do with Herne the Hunter," I hazarded, but I wasn't sure if that was right.

"I'll look it up."

"Yeah, we probably have a book about it. Dilys will know."

"I meant online."

We staggered on and I didn't reply to that.

***

Maddie had another half day of work in Sian's shop the next morning. I had some people to visit with my various remedies, including a rabbit with itchy eyes, a shopkeeper with bad feet, and a young mum who just desperately needed sleep, vodka, babysitters, adult conversation and a damn good cry.

The storm had raged all night. The crisp, pristine whiteness of the snowy verges were now scarred by debris. Smaller branches had been torn from trees, and people's bins had been scattered down the streets. Signs had gone over, and litter had bunched itself into random corners.

I left young Katie, the exhausted mum, just before midday. It had been a little early to suggest the vodka to her but I'd filled her freezer with easy-to-microwave food, filled her fridge with finger-food and snacks that could be dipped into even if they got cold (I was pretty sure she never got the time to eat a whole hot meal) and played with the sweet, fat baby while she indulged in a bath. Her family weren't around and the father was a taciturn long-distance lorry driver, who'd used up his holidays to be with them after the birth and was now on a mission to earn as much money as possible for his beautiful family. This meant he was never home. I wondered what Katie needed most. Cash or company?

I didn't know a great deal about babies, and I also wondered at what age she could start letting other people help out. Family babysitting was one thing, but could I enlist Jemima's help, I thought. There had to be something, some kind of support, out there for her. I was musing on this as I crossed the market square. It was busy and I realised that of course it would be, it was a Saturday.

That's the thing about being self-employed. You totally lose track of days. Adam was working this morning, and I hadn't really clocked it as being the weekend, even though later on we were off to that high ropes place for our sort-of-not-a-date. There were kids around, kicking up the snow and screaming at one another in delight.

Then I spotted the little cloud of teenage hormones that were our resident "gang" – the actual size of the group varied but there was a central core of three, led by sixteen-year-old Lacey. I knew she had younger brothers and sisters, and decided to ask if she was ever interested in babysitting. I wandered over to the bench that they were lounging on.

Lacey was tall and rangy, like she hadn't yet grown into her body yet, or else was going to end up as a supermodel. She was dressed entirely in black, and even her hair was dyed a deep midnight shade. She had a remarkable way of doing her make-up that made me envious, which I tried hard to not let change into judgmental. She was very different to how I'd been as a teenager – she was dramatic, loud, and confident.

If I had been in her class at school, I think I would have ended up more like the silent Kelly who was perched on the far end of the bench. In between Kelly and Lacey was Eira, who seemed to be Lacey's second-in-command. She, too, dressed in black but her make-up wasn't quite as polished.

"Hey, Lacey," I said, trying not to feel intimidated by her cool gaze. I was an adult, I reminded myself.

She looked me up and down. She didn't smile. But she did at least speak. "S'mae, Bron."

"So, uh, do you ever do any babysitting?"

She blinked very slowly. "No. I hate children. I'd eat them. Why?"

"Ah. Not even for money?"

"Not even for money. Would rather stick pins in my eyes. Why?"

Rude, I thought. "Well, obviously, because I had some potential babysitting work."

She stared pointedly at my stomach, though I was wearing enough clothes that I could have been eight months gone with twins and you would not have noticed. "That copper finally got his end away, has he?"

Rude, rude, rude. Ahh, teenagers. "Could have been him, could have been one of a dozen other men," I said airily, pleased by my witty comeback.

But Lacey sneered and her hench-women sniggered. "Been around a bit, have you? Didn't think that of you. Wow. Ha … well done."

Ah, yeah, I realised too late that it didn't matter what I said, it would be spun the opposite way. Lacey won these battles because of how she said things, not what she said.

No more cool retorts came to mind, and that was probably for the best. I said haughtily, "Well it's actually none of your business. So, uh, anyway. That's a no to the babysitting? Let me know if you change your mind." I turned away.

As I did so, Eira, who was staring at her phone, let out a muffled curse. "Screen's died again."

I stepped away. That was me, due to my embarrassment. I just needed to put some distance between us and her mobile would spring back into life again. I rarely damaged anything permanently. While I'd been at Katie's house, her television had randomly turned itself on and off. It was annoying, but temporary.

But Lacey knew. She said, "Hey, that's you, isn't it?"

I turned back to face her, but stepped away a few more paces. "Yeah, sorry. Look, I'm going now."

"No, wait."

Eira looked up with a scowl. "Hey, no! I'm trying to message someone. Tell her to cock off."

Lacey tipped her head. She leaned forward, and dropped her voice but I could still hear her. "What's the deal with Gruffydd?" she asked. "You're his friend, right?"

At first I thought she was referring to his sexuality. But, while he didn't exactly take out an ad in the local paper, most people knew he was gay. I narrowed my eyes. "I am his friend, yes, but there is no 'deal' with him. What do you mean?"

"My ma sent me to see him yesterday to pick up some shit she had him make for dad," she said, rolling her eyes to convey her artificial disdain for any hint of a relationship between her parents. "So I went up, like, but I saw something and the storm was coming and I … didn't go in. What's he up to, there, then?"

"Come on, Lacey, you're going to have to be a little bit more specific than 'saw something'. Don't you do English composition at school?"

"School sucks."

"Actually you're one of the brightest kids and I saw your photo in the paper last week for winning that chess competition, so knock it off. What made you so suspicious?"

She beckoned me closer. Eira huffed but she put her phone away, and we all leaned in to listen to what Lacey had to say.

"There was a huge man there, waiting in the yard, with horses and dogs around him," she said. "I think that's what I saw. Everything seemed to be moving really quickly. And there was the snow, and it ... just went really dark, like you know, in an eclipse or something. This man, he was enormous, but it was his ... uh, hat? Or maybe it wasn't a hat. He had, like ..."

Her eyes were large. I realised she was scared. She was reliving the emotions she had felt when she had seen the figure. I sent her some psychic reassurance. I crouched down and she hunkered forwards. "He had *antlers*," she whispered. "And don't you dare ask if I was high. I wasn't then. I was about thirty minutes later, though. *Obviously*."

Now was not the time to lecture her on her lifestyle choices, and for all I knew she was bluffing anyway, about the drugs. Instead, I nodded, and said, "I believe you totally." I knew exactly what she had seen. "He was shoeing the Wild Hunt," I told her, "and you did the right thing in walking away. It will not harm you."

"Are you sure?"

"I promise. It's not of this world but it won't have anything to do with you, as long as you don't mess around on the edges of things."

She was still scared. "And if I do mess around?" Her eyes flickered sideways. Eira and Kelly were looking equally petrified.

"What have you been up to? Ouija boards, that kind of thing?"

"Maybe."

"Well, don't, unless you are being guided by someone older and more experienced who knows what they are doing."

"Could you…?"

I stood up. "So, about that babysitting?"

She curled her lip. "Yeah, all right, let me talk to my ma about it."

"Excellent."

I grinned. I decided not to push my luck in making her concede any more to me, and I waved at Eira. "Okay, I'll let you get on with your texting."

"Snapchat, actually."

"Right, of course." I didn't have a clue what she meant. I turned but then remembered that these kids spent all their time hanging around, watching the town go about its business. "One last thing. Seeing as we are getting on so well and all that. Have you heard of a stone circle around here?"

They stared at me blankly.

"You'd know," Lacey said.

"Yeah, I would, wouldn't I? Yeah. Sorry. And do you know anything about Edmund Tait and Chloe Davies?"

They all shook their heads. "Chloe just lost her fella. She'll be off back to London or Liverpool or wherever. Tait's just a farmer. His family's one of the weird ones."

"Weird? You mean old, right?"

Lacey nearly smiled. "I thought you knew all this," she said.

"I'm just a healer."

"Huh, really?" She looked like she didn't believe me. "His family are all like you."

"They are not healers. I'd definitely know that."

"No, I mean, woo-woo. Magic," she said, adding a little giggle to suggest that she wanted to believe, she did believe, but also wanted to seem superior and above it all. "They do things up near their farm in that really small field. It's got three hawthorns in the middle of it, and never any sheep."

"Things?"

Now all three were giggling. "You know, *things*. At night."

I wasn't sure what field they were talking about. "Cheers," I said. "I'll be in touch about the babysitting."

"When are you due?" Lacey asked. "Cos I thought you were just fat."

They cackled with laughter, and I let them have the victory. But I sent a quick blast of energy towards Eira's hands which were already cradling her phone again. That should see it mangled for about an hour, I calculated.

Petty, but fun.

***

I walked away, heading for the shop where Maddie would soon be concluding her shift. I stopped at the door, and peered through the glass. It looked relatively busy, and I shuddered to myself. I really had no time for knick-knacks and twee ornaments of big-eyed fairies sitting on rocks. I was also uncomfortable with what I perceived as cultural appropriation – all the "native" dreamcatchers and things – not to mention the dubiously-mined crystals. Were things really more powerful or spiritual if they came from further away?

Sian was there, and I shrank back. She was so fluffy and light, and there was something about her that didn't sit right with me. I had recently come to understand that it was her deep reliance on the glamour she learned from the Faeries – the real ones, not the pretty fakes on toadstools – and that was the reason Maddie was working there. She was learning under Sian. It didn't matter that I couldn't stand Sian. She was the most knowledgeable one for Maddie, and that would keep Maddie safe – I hoped.

I felt a little sad as I watched them. They laughed together, and spoke with animation to a customer who was clutching a plaster goat's head.

It was good that Maddie was getting to know other people.

I backed away. I decided I wouldn't meet her after her shift. She wasn't expecting me, anyway.

Instead, I headed back home. I had an hour to get ready before Adam picked me up for our date.

NINE

I was looking forward to doing something totally different. We could have chosen better weather for our outdoor expedition, but to be honest, we could have chosen a Wednesday in June and still had to have worn jumpers and fleece coats. So I dressed warmly and then spent some time in the utility room, the back door propped open, seeing to my animals.

I had become engrossed in communing with a beautiful polecat when something jerked at my awareness and I realised that it was twenty minutes past the time that Adam had said he'd pick me up.

I persuaded Fitch the polecat to undulate back into his cage – he was much better now and nearly ready to go home to his doting owner, Frank – and wandered out to the front of the house. I looked up and down the quiet road but there was no sign of Adam.

I went back inside and braced myself to use the landline phone. I picked it up and it began to buzz. I fought my natural energies, drawing myself into a small psychic circle, but as I was about to dial, the back door rattled.

"Hey! Adam!"

"Hey. I'm sorry I'm so late," he said, only poking his head around the door frame.

"Come in."

"I won't." He looked very sheepish. "Prince was ill. Everywhere," he added ominously.

"What? Is he okay now? Do you need me to come and see him?"

"No, and perhaps," Adam said. "But we're supposed to be going out…"

"Rubbish," I said. "I'm ready. Take me to your place."

"Wow, I love a forceful woman."

I stepped into the utility room and stepped back into the kitchen again, holding my hand to my nose. "And I love a man covered in dog sick… couldn't you have changed?"

"I did. Twice. But you know what Prince is like…"

I promise you, I have never met a more vindictive poodle in all my life. "I do." I tried not to breathe as I followed Adam out to his car, and I rode with my head out of the window.

***

Adam explained the issue to me as we drove over. I could mostly hear him, in spite of the wind in my left ear. Prince was his parents' dog and he looked after it from time to time. His parents had followed him to Wales from their home in Zambia a few years ago. Prince was a tall, rangy poodle with a sharp nose and a huge sense of entitlement. I hate to allocate political leanings to animals, as they ought to be above all that, but if Prince could have spoken, he would have sneered at people who didn't drive the right sort of car. He was that kind of dog.

But even a snobby poodle can be fallible, and Prince had proved too clever for his own good. He'd got into the kitchen as the doors had lever handles, and he'd even got into a cupboard, and then he'd got into a box of chocolates and that was where it had all gone wrong.

I listened to Adam's words but I was also listening to how he spoke. Not just his accent, but the timbre of his voice.

I could see why he loved being a policeman. He was capable and responsible, and he seemed to thrive on being capable and responsible. He calmly outlined what he'd done when he'd come home to find the evidence of Prince's adventures. He'd called the vets, of course, and alerted them that he was on his way. He didn't waste time doing anything else. He just got the dog to the best place for him.

That had been last night. But since then, Adam explained, Prince had been "not quite right." Of course he'd been straight back down to the vets, who could find nothing else wrong.

And dogs were often sick, and Prince had done the usual dog thing of dealing with the sick himself, before Adam had had a chance to get to it, leaving nothing but a smelly stain on the rug and, in one case, Adam's trousers.

"I was late because I was trying to settle him," he explained. "But the vets are stumped and so am I. They suggested you, as it happens."

Doctors must have to deal with patients they didn't like, I

thought, so I can deal with Prince. Still, I walked into Adam's flat slowly.

As soon as I saw the poodle, my antipathy vanished. I made my way carefully into the room and regarded the dog from the corner of my eye. Adam breezed past behind me and went to the kitchen, saying, "Anything you need?"

"I'll let you know." I knelt down, about three feet away from the dog, and began to cast a circle around myself.

I extended the circle and invited the dog to join me in a safe space. He crawled his way forwards and came to rest alongside me, his head on my thighs. I closed my eyes and felt for the source of his distress.

When I started to laugh, Adam came running in from the other room. "What? What on earth?"

I was bending forward, my forehead almost touching the dog's head. I wouldn't usually advise anyone to put their face in a dog's face but he invited me in. I sat up as Adam approached.

"The great idiot is just sulking," I said.

"Excuse me?"

I scratched the poodle's neck and he leaned against my hand. "How long are your parents away for?"

"I didn't tell you they were away."

"You didn't need to. He did. He's pining, that's all."

"But the chocolates?"

"The crappy brown icing on the turd cake of life. Basically he was feeling sorry for himself before and the whole stomach-pump incident has knocked him for six. He just wants to be at home with his little pack of three. No offence, but you just aren't the same."

Adam put his hands on his hips. "What a baby."

"They do say a dog's about the same level, emotionally, as a toddler."

Adam sighed. "I am so sorry."

"It's okay," I told him, getting to my feet. "You didn't know. But he'll be fine as soon as your folks are back. Which is…?"

"Tomorrow. No, I mean, I am sorry about our date. Our booked session started half an hour ago. We can't make it."

I took his hands in mine. "Not even if you use the sirens and blue flashy lights?"

He grinned. "You know I can't."

"Well, we'll have to entertain ourselves here somehow."

"I've got no food in."

"Damn," I said. "So we'll have to have pizza?"

"I am sorry," he said again.

"It's okay. I will suffer eating lovely, yummy, delicious, non-clean food this once. Grab the menus."

He smiled back at me. "You are special."

***

When I got back late that night, everyone else was in bed. I remembered to remove the food that Maddie had left out for her Faerie friends, and went up to bed quickly myself, still smiling.

The next day, I headed out to see Gruffydd in his forge. It was a warm and welcoming place on this cold day, and I knocked the snow from my boots at the door as he waved at me and shouted, "I'll put the kettle on, shall I?"

"Please."

Everything in his workshop seemed to have a grubby mark or dirty handprint on it, and his once-white plastic kettle was no different. I wandered over to his small kitchen area. "Shouldn't you really have a big black pot hanging over a fire or something?" I said.

"Shouldn't you have a wolfskin wrapped around your shoulders and a trail of rats following you?"

"I beg your pardon? Are you saying I attract rats, like I smell of rotten food or something?"

"No, you idiot, I mean, like you and animals and your shaman stuff."

"I am not a shaman and you know it."

He grinned. He had one of those big strong jaws like you see in comics on the heroes, and sandy-blond hair that flopped a little over his forehead. He wasn't some great muscular hunk of a man, though he was very strong, in a sinewy sort of way.

"Pull up a pew, then," he said. "What's occurring?"

I took the smeared cup from him and sat back on one of the rickety chairs. "Oh, this and that. Mostly, I was wondering about the Wild Hunt."

"Oh, yeah, well, he passed over last night. You would have heard them, yeah. Good times."

"What do you know about it?"

He scratched at his jaw and regarded me thoughtfully. "A little of this, a little of that. Same as you, perhaps."

"Well, no, I don't think so. I've heard of it but no one has ever really spoken of it. I've never encountered it on my journeys. It's not my kind of magic. But you are a horse-man so …"

"Okay. There are some things I can tell you. I would say that it's led by Arawn and I'd call it the Cŵn Annwn."

"You *would* say?"

"Others would say different. Woden, Herne the Hunter, even Arthur. Regardless of his name, he is the King of the Wild Hunt. There are other riders but all are in thrall to him, and everything is about the hunt and the chase. And they say that it is a bad omen."

"To the person who sees it? Or just generally?"

"Either, really."

"You seem very relaxed about it. I found it…" But I tailed off. I felt as though I ought to say "terrifying" but the truly terrifying thing was, it hadn't been terrifying at all. It had filled me with an exhilaration that I found scary but that was my reaction to my own feelings – not the Hunt itself.

"You found it…?"

"I don't know," I said lamely. "So it's not an evil thing, then?" I knew it wasn't already but I needed reassurance.

He laughed. "No, it really isn't, though some will tell you so. They are not the dogs of Satan or any such thing. I don't even say it is a bad omen. You know your Mabinogion – you know that Annwn is not hell, not like the Christian hell."

"Have you ever … met this King?" I asked hesitantly. I didn't want to get Lacey into trouble for spying, though she hadn't been, not really.

He was still very laidback. "Yes. I shoe his horse, of course."

I had known it.

In spite of the heat from the forge and the cup of tea in my hands, I shivered. That flippant sentence reminded me that Gruffydd worked with an old magic and a powerful one of fire and iron and horses, and it was one that I had no idea about.

I tried to laugh lightly. It sounded forced to me. "Ahaha, yes, you shoe the King of Annwn's horse, yes, of course you do. Do you make small talk with him?"

He met my gaze but my levity was not reflected in his expression. "And you skirt around the edges of Annwn, at least, on your journeys at night, and *I* have seen *you* pass overhead. Do you make small talk with *Her*?"

Ouch. Point scored. I looked down at my cup of tea. "Gross. Do you ever wash your cups?"

"No. The build-up of tannin adds to the flavour. It makes a stronger, deeper brew."

"Seriously, you could put hot water in this cup and there's enough stain on the side to make a cup of tea without the use of a teabag."

"Exactly. I think it's good budgeting and household management."

"Minging."

I drained the dregs of the tea anyway. I mean, come on. Tea is tea. We both stood up at the same time. He grabbed my hands and gave them a squeeze.

"You are okay, though, *cariad*?"

"I am, thanks. Yeah. Sorry about the intrusive questions."

"That's ok. You didn't ask me the important ones."

"Really? What should I ask?"

"Oh, you know, friend stuff…" He was trying to hold back a grin.

I literally squealed. "You're dating someone! Who is he who is he who is he?"

"Calm down, calm down." But he wasn't calm either – I could see the delight in his eyes. "He's called Josh and he's an engineer who's working here for a few months on secondment from the head office of his company."

"Is he lovely?"

"Of course he is. And how is it going with Adam?"

"Not bad."

"If that is the best you can say… not *bad*…"

"I have been so busy," I said. "And there's other stuff going on in my head right now. But we're planning on going on some outdoor adventure thing soon." We just hadn't ever got around to rearranging the date, I remembered.

"Keep the momentum going," he said. "I know you two are good friends as well as dating, which is good. Just don't start taking one another for granted. Not so early in the relationship, anyway."

"I know, I know. Anyway, thanks for the tea."

"What's the other stuff on your mind?" he said, not letting go of my hands.

"Nothing. Oh, I worry about Maddie and her involvement with the Faeries."

"Don't. They will look after her."

"I worry about Dilys. She's not so young any longer. What

if…?"

"Don't," he said. "You know of death more than most. I won't give you any easy platitudes but you will be strong enough when the time comes."

"I worry about the man who was killed…"

"Killed? No, he died of an accident. Or do you know differently?"

"It can't have been an accident. Have you encountered anything strange – otherworldly, I mean, that isn't usually around?"

"No, not at all. The Hunt is common enough, for a start."

"Nothing else?"

He pressed my hands again. "No, nothing aside from the usual round of spectres and beings that I always encounter. *Pwca, ceffyl dŵr*, the *gwyllgi* from time to time."

Shapeshifters, water horses, the dog of darkness. I wondered if that last one could have been what I'd seen on the spot where Hudson had fallen. "Where does the *gwyllgi* usually roam?"

"Roads and highways, and he pops in here some nights." When Gruffydd grinned then, I saw a darker light in his eyes. "He likes his ears scratched."

"Right." I shuddered.

"You know I am here for you, anytime. Call me, send a message, call around."

"Thank you. I will. Although maybe not when you've got the actual dog of darkness prowling around."

"Oh, he doesn't prowl. He's much more of a lumberer, to

be honest. Quite lazy when he's not … you know. Doing his other stuff. The night terror stuff."

"Still puts me off. Catch you later. *Hwyl*."

"*Hwyl*."

***

The snow was holding off. I crunched my way along the frozen stuff that had previously fallen, and decided I needed to go back to the town and see if Maddie was still at work. I would walk home with her, after all.

I was happy that Gruffydd had met someone but it worried me that the guy was only here on secondment. That was temporary – what would Gruffydd do? If things worked out between them, would he ever consider moving away?

I tried to imagine doing what Maddie had done. Could I completely uproot myself and start again somewhere new?

I couldn't imagine moving out of the house I'd always lived in, not even if I stayed in Llanfair. I tried to picture how it would be. I couldn't. I was tied to it.

And I realised I was not normal.

I didn't pursue that train of thought. I'd reached the shop but I could see only Sian in there, at the counter, alone.

I must have missed Maddie. I turned around and set off across the market square.

"Hey! Bron! Coo-ee!"

I waved at my cousin who was emerging from Caffi Cwtch, holding a paper bag which she tried to hide behind her hip.

"Oho? Still eating clean, are we?" I mocked.

"It's a treat for all of us," she said as she fell into step beside me. "Heading home?"

"Yeah. You done for the day?"

"I am. I wanted to pop to the library after my shift to send some emails home and catch up on Facebook, but it had closed by the time I left the shop. That's how I ended up in the café, using up all the data on my phone. I tried sitting outside but I froze half to death."

She didn't need to add, "because of your curse preventing me from having internet at home like the rest of the civilised world." I could feel the recrimination, I was sure of it.

What would it be like to leave home, I wondered again.

TEN

We walked on and I sank into a self-pitying gloom which was instantly dissipated when Maddie said, "Oh, and I asked Sian about the stone circle, too."

I stopped dead. "Is there really one around here?"

"She says so, but it's not something you can see from the outside."

I folded my arms. But then we started walking again, and I realised I looked an idiot for walking along with my arms folded. I let them drop and I said, in a patronising tone, "You know, the thing about stones is – and maybe it's different in America, I don't know – but the thing about stones is, you can actually see them from the outside. What with them being all solid and, you know, *stoney*."

"Yeah you're cute," she said, completely unoffended. "The stones are small and just lodging low in the ground. That's why you can't see it until you are on top of them. The whole point of it is, though, is that it's a sacred place."

"How so?"

"It's where seven ley lines converge. It sounds pretty cool.

We should go check it out."

"And where is this mystical place of great power that I have never heard of before?" I asked.

"Um, so she did tell me, but I can't remember."

"You mean, you can't pronounce it."

"That too."

I spun around on my heel. "Let's go back and ask her. This has got me intrigued."

***

"Be nice," Maddie cautioned me as we stepped into Sian's palace of hippy tat.

I fully intended to. I really did.

But Sian Pederi was everything that rubbed me up the wrong way.

We started well. In that, I let Maddie do the talking at the beginning and I stayed quiet.

"Where was that stone circle you told me about?" Maddie said.

Sian Pederi had big, bright pink hair with grey roots, and earrings that could carry a week's shopping, and feathers and flowers not just in her hair but randomly stuck to her multi-coloured homespun cardigan. I doubted it was truly homespun. It looked expensively awful and a real home craftsperson took a lot more pride in their work. Sian Pederi didn't see the point in working hard to craft one's own esoteric items when half a week's wages could see you walking home with Mystical Amulets and

Folding Altars and Precious Stones of Power and the gods knew what else.

And the smell gave me a headache. Honestly, if you were going to use incense, go right ahead – just, you know, choose one appropriate for the task. Not every damn fragrance going and especially not that "marijuana" one because who on earth wants to attract attention like that?

Well, apart from Lacey and her gang, I suppose.

Sian smiled widely and, to my eyes, falsely. I could not work out whether it was my own antipathy to her that made me think she was fake, or whether she really was fake, or whether it was some combination of that and her glamour. For of course, she worked closely with the erratic and arrogant Tylwyth Teg.

"Oh, so you told Bronnie about this?"

"Bron," I corrected her.

"I am *so* sorry sweetheart, don't you mind me, now, my love. Yes, yes, the stone circle. You know, I am surprised you don't know where it is already, though?"

"Maddie said they weren't visible and that they were on some ley lines," I said. "I don't really deal with ley lines."

Her thin, drawn-on eyebrows wiggled. I felt judged, as if to be considered properly magical, I should know all about them. "Well, they are a very important source of earth power," she said.

I bit my tongue.

Maddie stepped in. "I totally forgot the name of the place you said, Sian." She smacked her forehead dramatically.

"Pen Madoc," she said.

"Oh! I do know that hill," I said. And I kept to myself the

next thing: it was up near the Tait's farm.

The Taits, who performed strange rituals, according to Lacey. Up there at their farm, where there was a field with three hawthorns where there was never any sheep.

Edmund Tait was looking more and more suspicious. His name kept on cropping up at the moment. Okay, so this wasn't really connected to the death of Hudson, but it seemed too much of a coincidence. I didn't necessarily believe in the universe giving us mortals clear signs – I reckoned the universe was too busy just being the universe – but I *did* recognise that our unconscious minds knew far more than we were aware of, and these snippets of information would float to the surface and look like serendipity.

"But where exactly is the circle?" I asked.

"Oh, I can't really describe it in words," she said airily. "I follow the lines, you see. Have you not read The Old Straight Track?" Her eyes flicked towards one of the shop's bookshelves.

I wasn't about to be sold to. "Yeah, we have an original copy at home," I told her. Okay, it was a facsimile reprint, not quite original, but hey.

She smiled broadly. "There you go, then! Have a read of that. I would come and show you right now, of course, but I can't leave the shop. You know how it is. Work work work! Well, obviously, it is *different* for someone like you…"

"How so?" I said, my voice dropping. There must have been menace in it, because Maddie put her hand on my arm. I wrenched my arm out of her grasp. I was having none of her glamour, not today.

Perhaps it was the cloying incense which was getting to me.

"This shop is such a responsibility and I feel very strongly, as a small business owner that is part of the beating heart of the town, that I must make myself as available as possible, you know? It's all to do with balance. Although I give so very deeply of myself, I know that I am rewarded in the most wonderful ways. Service is its own reward, in a sense, of course. But as I say: balance. I must balance that with my need to buy food and so on, and there is no shame in asking the universe to bring wealth…"

"You're talking about three or four different things all at the same time," I said snippily, "and half of them are total–"

"Bron!" Maddie grabbed my arm and pulled me backwards. This time I could not pull free.

"No, I mean asking the universe to–"

"We're off!"

"Yeah, balance and stuff, I can agree with, but the idea that you can just demand–"

"Thanks *so* much, Sian. See you soon!"

I was hauled out into the street.

"Good heavens," I said, and added a few more curses to make Maddie frown. "What's with the cosmic vending machine stuff?"

"You were just looking for something to pick a fight with her about," Maddie said.

"I wasn't. She was! She started it, all that 'ooh I am a real business' stuff. It was a dig at me. Come on, it was obvious."

"Maybe she's jealous."

"Of what?" I scoffed. "She's daft in the head. And exploitative."

"Do you think she's exploiting me?"

"No, but she sells crap to people when they really don't need it."

"And so do I."

"Yeah but … you're learning about important stuff."

"From her, the woman you've just insulted, who was trying to help us, in her own way."

"She couldn't even tell us where this bloody thing is!"

"She told us enough," Maddie said. "If you can get us up to the right area, I can probably pick up enough on the ley lines to zone right in on it."

I hesitated. I wanted to carry on arguing, and I knew that was pretty stupid and petty.

"Okay, then," I conceded at last. "The more we hear Edmund Tait's name, the more suspicious I get of that man, and his family. So let's go up and have a look at his parents' farm, and check out this circle on the way."

"Are you going to go back into the shop and apologise to Sian?"

I made my eyes into slits and flared my nostrils. "Just as soon as I sprout wings and start sitting on clouds playing a harp," I said grimly. "Let's go."

ELEVEN

The farm that belonged to the Tait family was very different to the one that Gordon and Lynn ran. We knew we were getting close by the sight of piles of rubbish littering the side of the rutted, pitted track. The stone walls around the fields were in bad repair, crumbling and with great holes that were blocked off with barbed wire and electric fences.

The fields were rough and scrubby. Each one contained an old bath of water, and metal feeders surrounded by a sea of churned up mud and snow.

As the land rose, the fields opened out, and we were on open moorland now, where their sheep were able to graze at will. The cold air scratched its talons down my face and I could smell the bitterness of snow in the atmosphere.

I pointed up to the left. "That's Pen Madoc," I said. "The hill there."

"Right, so we're looking for a field with three hawthorns, did you say?" Maddie said. "I think you're right, that's the most likely kinda spot. And we need to feel for the leys."

"What do they feel like?" I asked as we took turns to

clamber over a slippery stile.

"I'm not *so* great at detecting them yet," she confessed. "But when I do, they feel like a … uh, I dunno, a sparkling throb deep inside my head?"

"Let me know if you feel that. I want to see if I can get it, too."

If there was a path to follow, it was hidden under a few inches of snow. We struck out across the blank whiteness. Up ahead, I could see a few wandering walls marking erratic field edges, and a handful of small clumps of trees.

"That's it," I said. There was an enclosure that looked very out of place and right in the middle there were three small stunted trees. I would not have noticed it if I had not been looking. "We don't need to follow the ley lines. It's obvious now." I started forward, but she didn't follow.

Maddie was looking around. "Seven lines are supposed to cross here," she said. "Each of them will link up with other sacred or powerful sites. I need to learn to dowse, so I can pick up the earth energies more easily."

She closed her eyes and extended her hands, drawing in on herself. I stepped to one side to let her do whatever it was she was doing.

She looked like she was sniffing the air, jutting her chin up as she took tentative steps forward.

I was impatient to get to the stone circle, not that I could see any stones yet. But when Maddie called out, "Here's one!" I raced to her side and tried to feel the same thing.

The hairs lifted on the back of my neck, but I could not

have sworn that I was definitely feeling any ley line. After all, I was expecting to, and what we expect to see has a powerful bearing on what we do see. Or detect. Or feel.

But Maddie could clearly feel something. With her eyes still closed and her chin almost skyward, she now stepped forward confidently, following a direct line up the hill, tramping through the snow.

She would have marched straight into the field, were it not for the fact that she collided with the stone wall and winded herself.

I doubled over with laughter, and she whipped around. "You could have told me I was about to walk into a wall!"

"Why? Watching you do it was too funny. And also a learning experience."

"What did I learn? To not trust you?"

"No," I said, more seriously. "To temper whatever you learn through magical means with everyday rationality." I was impressed. I sounded like Horatio.

She opened her mouth to retort, and then closed it again. She nodded.

I marked that one up as a victory to me – ooh, the pettiness! – and together we went over the wall and into the small, irregular shaped field. Open land surrounded us. We padded up to the hawthorns and then fanned out, exploring the ground. I scuffed at the snow with my boot, and this time it was my detection of earth energies that was successful.

Something deep below us pulsed and I knew I had it. I kicked away the snow and there it was – buried half in the ground.

I could not tell whether I was looking at the tip of a massive monolith, or it was just a football-sized rock.

But once we had this one, we could trace the circle and we counted thirteen more, which fitted. There are thirteen full moons in a year, after all.

"Well," I said, "you were right all along. About this, at any rate."

"Is that an apology?" Maddie grinned.

"It's a … concession." I grinned back.

"Can I get you to sign this?"

"Oh, uh, my fingers are too cold right now."

"Sure, sure."

We stood in the centre and basked in our glory.

"Now what?" Maddie said. "I'm pleased we found the stone circle. And I guess this is where the Taits do their … whatever it is that they do. But we should head back, right? We actually don't have long left before dusk."

I rubbed my face. "Something is calling me to look closely at Edmund Tait. He was there with Hudson before he died. He works on farms around here, his own family's and others. He is a friend of Chloe's, who was Hudson's girlfriend. And his family is an old one who are said to conduct some kind of rituals right here. And Hudson's death is suspicious."

"So you think there was a magical connection to his death?"

"There has to be! He didn't fall from a quad bike. He wound up dead in the snow with impact injuries as if he fell from a great height…" I tailed off and stared at Maddie in horror.

"What is it?"

"Maddie," I whispered, "Gruffydd shoed the horse of the King of the Wild Hunt."

Her eyes widened as she understood my meaning.

Maybe Tait was nothing to do with any of this.

But Gruffydd…?

***

We hurried on up to the Tait's tumbledown farm. There were rusting pieces of farm machinery, rolls of wire, and blue barrels scattered alongside the track now, and up ahead of us, we could see the squat grey buildings that made up the farmstead. A dog was barking, but its heart wasn't in it. I could tell it had been barking for a long time, and it was no longer sure what it was even barking at.

Seeing to the dog became my immediate priority.

There was a rusted gate lodged in the mud, looped to the gatepost with frayed orange twine. We squeezed through and I went straight to where the dog, a shabby-looking collie, was tied up. She lunged at me, mad blue eyes staring wildly.

I didn't care if anyone was watching me or what they thought of my actions. I had a duty borne of my calling.

I stopped and stilled myself, and averted my eyes. I called up all the spirits around me and asked for help, casting a circle of invisible energy, letting my animal nature come to the fore.

I tuned out everything that was superfluous to this moment.

Now I could feel the dog's rapid, anxious heartbeat as clearly as if my head were pressed to her chest. I brought it into line with my own; slower, deeper, more powerful.

I could feel her becoming calmer, and I flicked a glance her way. Now she was standing still, watching me warily, her head cocked, questioning.

I sent energy her way, warm and healing. She whimpered, and quivered, and now I could see what was wrong. She was old, of course. And I knew what she needed. And it was what we needed, too, in a sense.

I blinked and shook myself, and turned to Maddie. "Right. We're going in."

I rapped on the wooden door until it opened. I stared down into a pair of pale blue eyes, and I recognised the old face of Mother Tait.

She had not spoken for four years or more, so the gossip went. Perhaps she was ill, or stubborn, or had simply run out of things to say. I detected no feeling of illness around her.

And I knew she could hear and understand. "*P'nawn da*, Mrs Tait," I said politely. "Might we come in?"

She raised her sparse eyebrows.

"It's about your dog," I said, smiling.

She frowned, but stepped back. I took it as an invitation to enter the farmhouse. We stepped through a dark, cold porch area and into an equally dark corridor that faded into nothingness at the far end. She backed into a kitchen and I was fully expecting there to be a blast of hot air as we entered, but in truth the atmosphere was barely temperate.

No wonder she appeared to be wearing her whole wardrobe at once.

There was a dark wood table piled high with Farmer's Weekly and *Y Tir*, stock books and paperwork with crinkled yellow edges. Unlike our house, there was no old-fashioned range. Instead there was a battered electric cooker, and covering all four rings at once was a huge aluminium saucepan. It smelled of lard and burned grease.

"Bronwen Talog," said a voice and I realised I'd missed the other person in the room. Mr Tait, Edmund's father, sat on a hard wooden chair next to a small fire that was giving off more smoke than heat.

"Mr Tait, sir, how are you?"

"*Da iawn*," he said, but he didn't look good. He had never looked good, for as long as I'd known him. Yet he'd never come to me for any healing, so I had to assume he was, in spite of appearances, perfectly well.

Mrs Tait sat down on another wooden chair. There were two other places to sit but both were piled with random objects and so Maddie and I both remained standing.

I hastily introduced Maddie but the couple looked almost bored with proceedings. Mr Tait half-nodded, and didn't say hello to Maddie.

I suddenly realised that we were going to need Maddie's glamour skills, if she could control the madness that it also brought. I slid her a sideways look. She caught my eye. I hoped it was enough to convey what I needed her to do.

"I have been developing a new remedy specifically for older dogs," I said. "It's based on golden paste, which I think most people know about, you know, turmeric and stuff, with some

113

additions of my own. But the thing is, I really need your help in testing it out and I wondered if your dog out there could possibly benefit? She is probably the right age. It would really help me."

Mrs Tait nodded a little, but Mr Tait sucked his teeth and drew in his grey cheeks so that his face became skull-like. "Seren's past it, to be honest with you. No point, see."

Seren is battling painful arthritis, you unfeeling clot, I wanted to say. But that was not the way to win this one, and I fought down my inclination to yell at him. "I am sure she has served you faithfully over the years. How old is she now?"

"Twelve, maybe. Thirteen? Don't know why we keep her to be straight with you. Costs in food, doesn't it."

You actually feed her? I kept that to myself. I had seen the ridge of her spine and while that wasn't unusual in an older dog, it still wasn't right. It didn't have to be like that.

Maddie stepped in. I felt the shimmering warmth of calm relaxation that heralded the use of her glamour, and I saw Mrs Tait visibly exhale, a long breath that she had probably been holding in, stressed and repressed, for years. Mr Tait blinked rapidly as he fought the unfamiliar feeling of happiness washing over him.

"How proud you must be," Maddie murmured. "What a fine dog who has now earned her rest and her comfort. Over a decade she has spent by your side!" Her sentences were more lyrical and her accent now mid-Atlantic, unplaceable. Maybe Atlantis was real and that was how they sounded there. That would fit.

I jerked myself out of my reverie. It was glamour-induced.

I had to keep a clear head. Maddie would be affected by her own magic if she used it for any length of time, and one of us needed to stay sane, as far as possible.

Mrs Tait was actually smiling, and nodding harder.

Mr Tait still fought it but he was crumbling as Maddie's magic delivered him memories of the times he'd spent with Seren. There was a bond between human and dog; but he had forgotten it. Maddie pushed it back into his heart once more.

"The thing is," I said quietly, "if you can help me out, that would be great, but I would have to provide the food for her to eat and it's quite important for her to be monitored so she'd have to be inside…"

Mrs Tait was now nodding frantically at her husband.

Mr Tait scratched his neck, running his finger around his collar and pulling at the cloth. "She don't have a job no more, though, now we don't have the sheep."

"She has earned a fine retirement, hasn't she? What a good dog, loyal all these years," Maddie said quietly.

"Well … she has, she has," Mr Tait said and I knew we had him. I pulled my backpack off my shoulder and fished around in it. I didn't have anything useful in there at all, but I did have a small plastic bag that contained some dried chicken and dog treats. It wouldn't do Seren any harm, and I'd call up to the farm again soon with the actual stuff to ease her aching joints.

In a daze, Mr Tait wandered outside and returned within a few moments with Seren at the end of a rope knotted about her neck. She snapped at us, but I calmed her and she hunkered down, licking her lips a few times before finally relaxing. Her eyes darted about and then she shook herself and trotted over to Mrs Tait, leaning against the old woman's legs for a hindquarter scratch.

While everyone was still under the influence, I decided now was the time to ask about Edmund and Chloe and David Hudson.

"I didn't realise you didn't run any sheep now," I said. "I see your son around still; is he not taking the farm over?"

"There's nothing here to take over," Mr Tait said morosely. "He'll do all right working for others. Less stress that way."

"But this farm has been here for generations," I said. "Like the Davies opposite … they are still farming, aren't they?"

Mr Tait looked away and shrugged. "All things end."

"I suppose so. That reminds me, did you hear what happened to Chloe Davies's boyfriend?"

"Fell, didn't he?"

"What from?"

Mr Tait shrugged again, and coughed, and looked back at me. The glamour was wearing off. "Just fell. Slippery up there. Got to be careful, see."

"Did you ever meet him?"

"No. No reason to. That the medicine for the dog, is it?" he said, pointing at the bag in my hands.

The conversation was over.

We had learned nothing.

Or could I shake the fog of glamour enough to be able to read between the lines?

I gave him the bag of treats with vague and meaningless instructions, and we left. Maddie was humming a silly little song to herself. I steered her out of the farmyard and back onto the track. Evening was closing in around us, and she was in a vulnerable state. The sky above us was darker than it should have been, and I could hear distant hoof beats. I looked up but there was no sign of the Wild Hunt.

Something screeched, far off behind us.

I grabbed Maddie's arm and dragged her home.

TWELVE

Our house was quiet and dark. I steered the still-soporific Maddie into an easy chair by the range, stoked it up, set the kettle on the top to boil and then went out to see to the animals. It was dark outside and bitterly cold, but the utility room where the injured creatures were recovering was a reasonable temperature. Not warm, but not freezing, at least. I hoped Seren was enjoying her new place inside, too. I stepped out into the back garden to look up at the sky and stars and moon for a moment, and nearly squealed when I bumped into the least likely figure to be found lurking there.

"Sian!"

"Oh, sorry. I didn't mean to make you jump. Bron, do you have a minute?"

"Sure." We stepped into the utility room. I would have taken her into the kitchen but she peeped through the half open door and saw Maddie slumped in the easy chair.

"I'll not disturb her. She been practising, has she, now?" Sian said, in a low voice.

"In a way. Did you want to see her? I can pass a message

on."

"No, no, you're all right. Actually it was you that I wanted to see."

I stared. She looked down and then up, and there was a hesitation in her voice. So, she hadn't come to continue the almost-argument we'd had, then. "Oh?" I said, as neutrally as I could. "How can I help?"

"Well, it's like this, see. Like I say, the shop is doing well, and everything. But I feel I have so much more to offer and it came to me in a dream, so you see, well, you understand, don't you?"

"Er … maybe? I dream about cheese a lot. And I eat a lot of cheese."

"What?"

"You haven't told me what your dream was about," I explained.

"Oh, yeah, so, the thing is, you see, I am going to open a spiritual retreat."

"Oh! I see."

Sian was nodding frantically. "Yes, and I thought, you being, well, specialised, as it were, you could help run some courses?"

"Courses about what?"

"Like I say, spiritual stuff. Mystical knowledge." And then she launched into the same spiel she was probably going to use in her promotion. "In this hectic modern world people are losing touch with what it means to be human but there is a growing awareness that we are intimately connected with the planet and one another and people are seeking to reignite the ancient wisdom which we once all knew."

"Er, yeah, I don't think I'm your best choice," I said. "I wish you all the luck in the world, but I just heal animals. And people."

She stared into my eyes and I wasn't comfortable. "No, Bron. I can see auras, you know, and yours is ... shimmering with violet and silver. You know what that means, don't you?"

Possibly that you're about to have a migraine, I thought. But I tried to smile. "I don't dwell too much on auras..."

"I'm sorry. We do move in different worlds but I really don't want you to think there's any kind of hierarchy, you know? I don't look down on you because of what you do. I don't mean the healing. I mean the other stuff. You're a hedge witch."

"I am a hedge rider," I said. "It's more than just collecting berries off a tree."

"I know, I didn't mean to insinuate anything else. But don't you see? That kind of rare knowledge would be so good for the retreat! People would love to hear more about that and learn to do a little themselves."

I wanted to say, "That is the worst idea I've ever heard. No, wait. It's just one step better than encouraging my cousin to explore her relationship with the Tylwyth Teg." I mean come on – this was not something you could do "do a little" of. Like weekend shamans or online diploma Satanists, this was not going to end well.

But I didn't say any of that. I thinned my lips and said, "I think I'd be a terrible teacher."

"Think about it. You'd be great. Mull it over. Meditate on

it and ask your spirit guides."

See, there's half the problem. I don't think what she meant by "spirit guides" was quite what the inexplicable reality was, at least for me. Still, I nodded. She meant well, and while she didn't understand my world, I didn't understand hers either. So we were equal. "I'll let you know."

She clapped her hands, cooed, and looked like she was about to air kiss my cheeks. I stepped back.

"Well, thank you," she said, and fluttered out into the night.

I spent a moment in the utility room, tickling the polecat. The woman was bonkers. Dangerously so, I thought uncharitably. But I had other things to worry out. I turned and went into the kitchen to ferret about in the freezers for something to eat.

I was just setting a spicy beef casserole to reheat when Dilys came in from outside, and she looked more tired than I'd seen her for a long time. She eased herself down, grunting, into the other easy chair, and tipped her head back, closing her eyes for a few moments.

Maddie, too, was dozing.

Harkin padded around, silently, and sniffed everyone's legs before making his own little nest on the rag rug by the fire.

The only sounds were the bubbling of the stew, and my aunt's rasping breathing. I could not hear anything from Maddie.

I poured another cup of tea for myself, and that brought Dilys's eyes open. She didn't need to speak. I added a few spoons of sugar and took it over to her.

"Aunt, are you all right?"

"*Diolch*," she said, thanking me for the brew. She took it by the handle and balanced it on the armrest of the easy chair. I leaned against the table and folded my arms.

"Dilys?"

"Oh – yes, yes, I'm fine," she said.

"You look tired. Can I get you anything?"

"I am tired. It's just been a long day."

"How so? I didn't think you had a fair today."

Something flickered over her face. "That's just it, you see," she said with a sigh. "I should have been at the Llangollen Mind, Body and Spirit event, but I missed out on the bookings. Just like last month when I didn't get a stall at Bangor."

"Why not? You've done Llangollen for years!"

"Elsie Delaney got in first and they said they didn't want two fortune tellers that were almost the same."

"That Delaney woman!" I said. "How did she manage to jump the queue?"

"Because they do all the bookings online now," Dilys muttered.

Damn. Damn and blast it.

I hunted around for something apologetic to say but before I could frame the words, Maddie had stirred. She wrinkled her nose and when I looked at her eyes, they seemed clear of enchantment. "Can I smell food?" she asked, back to her usual bright, cheerful American self again.

"You can. You can also butter some bread if you like."

"Sure."

The usual habits of an evening meal rolled on.

We were nearly done when there was a knock at the rear door. We all stopped and turned our heads, waiting for the visitor to simply invite themselves in and enter. That was the usual way – except for my friend Dean, who had a distinctive way of knocking that seemed to say "sorry" as he tapped away as quietly as he could. So this was not Dean. I wondered if Sian had returned.

They knocked again.

I got up and went through to answer it.

I was stunned to see Chloe Davies standing on the patio slabs.

"Oh. Hello, Chloe. Er … do you want to come in?"

She was dressed in black leggings, brown knee-high boots and a thick, warm-looking camel-coloured coat. Her make-up had been carefully done that morning, but the day had taken its toll. She looked smeared, rubbed and anxious.

"Yes, please. Thank you. Is it a good time?" She pushed her way in without waiting for an answer. I followed her into the kitchen.

Everyone stared.

Dilys started to stand up, but Chloe waved her down again. "Please, I didn't mean to interrupt your meal."

"Did you eat already?" Maddie asked, ever polite and welcoming. "There's plenty spare. Come on, sit down."

And so that was how Chloe Davies, one of the suspects – in my head, at any rate – came to be sitting and eating with us. I thought of the ancient laws of hospitality. She'd broken bread with us, quite literally. Did this mean we had to defend her with our lives now?

Was it a trick, I found myself thinking. Like vampires did. I've read *Dracula*.

I watched her carefully. She made polite small talk. Dilys asked how she had been – an innocuous question except that now we knew that Chloe had come to Dilys for advice.

Chloe said that she was tired, stressed and upset over recent events.

That was a perfectly normal thing to say, and she looked exactly how she described herself. She looked, in truth, just like a woman who had lost her boyfriend in tragic and unexplained circumstances.

Maddie jumped up to clear away and ordered us all to remain seated while she stacked the plates by the sink. I could not hold my tongue any longer.

"So, uh, Chloe, is this a social visit or can I … or my aunt … help you in any way?"

Chloe hung her head for a moment and fiddled with the silver rings on her fingers. Her shoulders were hunched and she looked very thin and cold. Then she clasped her hands together, drew in a deep breath, and looked up at me. Her eyes were swimming with tears.

I noticed all these things almost impartially, and I wondered if she was playing a part. I could feel strong emotion rolling from her, though, so something was definitely wrong.

"I was hoping that I might stay for a few nights."

Maddie dropped a fork.

Dilys coughed.

I stared.

Harkin jumped up into my lap and circled round a few times. I stroked him absently while I considered Chloe's words. Harkin was giving me no indication that I needed to be wary.

I looked over at Dilys before I spoke. She nodded at me. So, it was my decision, but my aunt already knew what I would say. It's what anyone would say when they were asked for help.

"Of course, Chloe. Anyone is welcome here in a time of need."

She sagged with relief. "Thank you!"

I glanced at Maddie. She nodded too. So we were all in agreement.

"However," I said, "I think it's fair for me to ask why. You have your own house or flat which might, I accept, currently be a difficult place to be. But your parents are local, and I am sure you don't lack for friends. I know you have old family links with the Taits, for example…"

"Yes – no," she said, shaking her head. "I just need to get away from *everyone* right now. I mean, my family, my friends, they're all lovely and they mean well but it's too much. I'm overwhelmed. I'd run off to a hotel somewhere for a week but I know that everyone would worry. I don't want people to worry about me, but I do want to be left alone."

"Of course," Dilys said, and I could feel my heart going out to her. How would I be reacting in her position? On recent form, I'd probably be attacking random people in the street and biting noses.

An uneasy silence fell. Maddie returned to washing the dishes, and Dilys got up and said she'd make a bed up in one of the small box-rooms upstairs. I remained where I was, stroking Harkin, and trying to tune into Chloe like I would connect with an injured animal.

She was fenced off. Completely and utterly closed off. It wasn't unusual – I'd felt that before when people were in the depths of grief, fear and confusion. Bereavement built walls around someone just when they needed such boundaries the least. It didn't mean she was deliberately shielding herself magically from me.

But as I bent my senses closer to her, I heard again that song, those fragmented words that had plagued my mind since my hedge riding recently. I wrenched my attention away from her, and the singing faded.

Almost, but not quite, it wafted out of earshot.

THIRTEEN

Maddie popped back downstairs to say she was going to bed, and bid us goodnight. The glamouring enchantment had taken its toll, especially as she had been fighting the less savoury effects. Dilys showed Chloe up to the room prepared for her, and I went out into the utility room to make some final checks on the animals. I gave more medicine to a malnourished kitten, and changed the bedding. The local vets had given me some drugs for her, and I was grateful for their donation, especially as the kitten was a stray. I'd bake them a cake to thank them, when I had time.

I locked the back door, and turned out the light, and nearly jumped out of my skin as I went back into the kitchen, because there was Chloe Davies again, just standing there in the gloom.

"Oh! Sorry, I thought everyone had gone to bed," I said. "You okay? Do you want a glass of water or anything?"

"Yes, please. Sorry, I don't know where anything is…"

I went to the cupboards and fetched her a glass. She filled it herself at the tap, but she didn't seem keen to leave.

"What's up?" I asked.

I probably sounded more terse than I meant to, because she winced. There was an apologetic note in her voice as she said, "Look, I know it's probably difficult for you to have me here…"

"No, it's fine, I'm sorry. I'm just surprised, that's all."

"Yes, of course."

"Look," I said, "about that other day in the street. I didn't mean to embarrass you or anything."

"No, you didn't. It was *him* doing the embarrassing."

"Your relationship seems – seemed to have been – stormy?" I asked.

"Yeah, you could say that." She sipped at the water, a pure displacement activity. "You want to know why I stayed with him, don't you?"

"Well, it's personal, so you don't have to talk about it if you don't want to," I said, very proud of my maturity, even if my inner drama-teenager was screaming *yes, come on, what on earth was wrong with you?*

She huffed, a humourless sort of laugh. "You're dying to know."

"You seem dying to tell me. If you want to talk about it, you can. Come on, have a seat."

We sat opposite one another at the table, but she didn't look up. I shoved my chair back so that I was at an angle, a less threatening position than head-on. She kept her hands clasped around the glass. "It's the usual tale," she said, her voice flat. "He didn't start out like that. And he was lovely, most of the time. And as long as I managed him right, everything was okay. And … I guess we were using one another, in a sense. I needed him and maybe I didn't leave him because it was easier to stay with him, you know. We were building a business together. And he'd been stressed, and he didn't handle stress very well. Who does?"

"And now he is gone," I said.

"So he is."

If I was expecting a sudden tearful confession, I didn't get it. I waited until she spoke again.

"Now he's gone," she repeated. "I do miss him. I shouldn't, should I? He was a nice man, kind to me, generous … but he was also a bully and sometimes, just sometimes, I was a bit scared of him. I'm all mixed up. I feel relieved and I also feel so … alone."

She began to cry.

I went to the sideboard and fetched a box of tissues, and this time I sat down beside her. I needed Maddie here to do this, really; she was the people-person, not me. I fixed bodies and I fixed animals, and in between times, I dealt with the otherworld. Everyday life was something of a mystery sometimes. I could barely work my own relationship out.

"Everything you are feeling is normal," I told her, carefully. "Well, there is no normal. You're having normal reactions to an abnormal situation. You can feel lots of things at the same time, you know. It's fine. *You* are fine."

She sniffed. "Thank you. I know. Everything will be okay but it comes in waves, these feelings. Then there's times when I don't feel anything at all and that's even worse. Am I a bad person?"

"No!" This time I even gave her a quick, one-armed,

sideways and awkward hug.

"Also, Bron … I'm scared."

"What of?"

She didn't answer for a long time and I had to check she hadn't passed out. I squirmed around in my chair and looked intently at her.

"What are you scared of?" I asked her again. "You know you are safe here."

"How do you think he died?" Chloe said in a whisper.

I shivered. "I was told he had fallen in the snow. He died in hospital, didn't he?"

"His injuries were too severe. Bron, you are so kind to let me stay."

"It's fine. Honestly. Anyone would do the same. You would, too."

"I suppose so. Everyone has been so very kind to me. I don't deserve it."

I wanted to press her further as to why she thought she didn't deserve it. I was starting to wonder if she could be the murderer. She had enough motive, that was for sure. But really? This crying woman? Could she have killed him?

But that would account for why she felt scared.

Why come here, though? Why not flee completely away?

Oh, but that would prove her guilt. Perhaps coming here was a good compromise. If she was guilty, she wouldn't want to stay near to people who knew her the best, would she?

"You do deserve it, I am sure," I said, cringing at my platitude. "You have many friends here who would agree."

"They've all moved on," she said. "I moved away and made a new life, and so did they. Coming back was a mistake. Everyone is different."

"Even Edmund Tait?"

"Why do you say that?" Suddenly her voice was stronger and the tears were gone.

"Oh, just that I know he's an old family friend," I said. "Okay, I'll be honest. I saw him in your new office and he looked out of place."

"He came to call and see how I was doing," she said. "Yes, you're right, his family and mine go way back." She laughed bitterly. "And we're supposed to go way forward, too."

"What's that supposed to mean?"

"Oh, that stupid thing our families always had," she said. "I thought everyone knew. It's the sort of thing that gossips love."

"I don't listen to gossips," I told her stiffly, while alarm bells began to ring in my mind. "What stupid thing?"

"They do rituals together, for the land," she said. "It's all nonsense."

"Is it?" I didn't want to break Dilys's confidence, but why would Chloe have visited my aunt if she didn't believe in the supernatural?

"Maybe there is something in it," she conceded. She sat back and put her hands into the pockets of the oversized cardigan she was wearing. She fiddled with something in the right hand pocket and she gazed off across the room. "Yeah, maybe there is something in it. My family have continued to do the rituals but the Taits, the old Taits, they stopped."

"Now their farm is gone," I said. But something didn't add up. Had the Taits stopped their rituals? Really? Lacey didn't think so.

"Indeed," Chloe said. "Their farm has died. Coincidence that it happened when they stopped the rituals and lost their connection? Probably. Still, you have to wonder."

"They do, or they did, these rituals at the stone circle?"

"Yeah, you know that place? Of course you do. Yeah, it's closer to the Taits' farm, but my family go there too."

The teen gang had seen the Taits there. Or had they seen Chloe's family? "Are you sure the Taits don't do any rituals now?" I asked.

"Mostly. Perhaps they've started again? I have been away. Edmund didn't mention it. Anyway…" She tailed off again, still distracted by whatever was in her pocket. "Anyway, yeah, the Taits. I don't like old uncle Tait. There's something about him."

"Uncle?"

"Yeah, that thing that the eldest Tait has to marry the eldest Davies. It's creepy and incestuous."

"Are you the eldest?"

She snorted. "Yes, I am, but it's just an old thing, almost like a joke, really. Ugh, I could never. Nope. No." Suddenly she pulled her hand free of her pocket. "I'd like to give you a gift."

"Er, what?" Her words had blindsided me – it was not at all what I'd expected to hear.

"I think it's the sort of thing you'd appreciate." She stood up and pushed the chair under the table, and put something down in front of us.

I looked at the thing on the table. "What is it?" It looked like a tangle of thin but coarse threads to me.

"It's a … well, it's made from horsehair, it's just an ornament."

"That's a weird sort of ornament."

"It's my way of thanking you," she said. "I don't have much else…"

Her bottom lip wobbled and I could not press her. She was in mourning, for heaven's sake – even I am not that heartless.

Before I could say anything else, she had gone.

And I was left in the darkened kitchen, staring with distaste at the loops of black and grey horsehair. I picked it up gingerly and let it dangle from my fingers. It made my skin crawl just to look at it. Magic rolled off it.

Had she known it was magical? If her family were magical, was she? She had not seemed so. I honestly didn't think there was a magical bone in her body.

I tested it for curses but there were none that I could detect. There was a magical power attached to it, but in day to day life, I often encountered things like this that non-magical people were blissfully unaware of. I remembered visiting a lovely old lady called Mavis who was using a deeply charmed prayer shawl as the rug in her cat's bed. The cat lived to twenty-three years old, and was never sick a day in its life.

So, it was possible that Chloe didn't know it was powerful. But it was a mighty strange gift to give anyone – I couldn't work out what it was.

I followed the threads by eye. There seemed to be three long horsehairs and they were knotted so that they fell in one large loop and one smaller one. Two long ends of horsehair dangled free.

It was no kind of ornament. It reminded me of knot-magic, and the charms you could make by tying and untying. Didn't they do this in childbirth when the baby would not come? Everything in the house had to be undone, and there had been cases of a malicious person hiding a knotted rope under the mother's bed to stop the birth being easy.

Perhaps it was that kind of magic.

My fingers hovered near a knot, but I stopped.

No. Until I knew what it was, and why she had given it to me, I would leave it as it was. Who knew what I'd release by undoing the knots? Harkin jumped up onto the table and sniffed it, and looked at me, and sat down to lick himself.

That settled it. If my cat was not overly concerned, then nor was I.

But I did not fully trust Chloe, and I knew she was not telling me the whole truth. Not about Hudson, not about the Taits, and certainly not about this object.

Had she given it to me just so she could be rid of it herself?

Fourteen

I left the house early the next morning. I had never really counted myself as much of a people-person. Until Maddie had turned up around Imbolc, I'd lived happily alone with just my aunt and my animals, and my handful of friends like Gruffydd, Dean and perhaps Horatio the vicar. I always told myself I didn't need any deeper relationships – I was secure in my place in my community, I knew everyone, and I had a job to do. I was content.

When Adam had sashayed into my life, it had taken a while to really acknowledge my feelings for him, and even longer to act upon them.

Then Maddie turned up and suddenly I was sharing my space in the house, and my space in the community, too. I had resisted the change. But she forced me outwards, telling me of the wider world beyond my own experience.

It was a world of technology and change, money and power, danger and hate and love and acceptance and I felt like I was some isolated and cloistered mediaeval nun sometimes when she spoke of the internet and smart phones and memes and message boards and emails and all the things I could never get to know, not properly.

Now there was yet another person in our house, and the energies were shifting once more. I didn't like it. I knew that I was simply overwhelmed by all the other chatter – internal and external – so I took myself away to recharge.

I also had a job to do. I'd made up various preparations that I felt would ease Seren the old sheepdog's aches and pains. I had a bag of food which weighed a ton, and I carried that in my arms with the medicines in my backpack to balance me out. Maddie had said she would organise a delivery of geriatric dog food up to the farm, via some internet wizardry. But this was to plug the gap before it was delivered.

It was coming up to *Gwyl Canol Gwenwynol*, which Maddie called Eostre and most non-magical folk called Easter. It was the most special time of year for my friend Horatio, the reverend. I wandered out past his church. The back of the churchyard bordered our gardens, but I went out along the path to the front, crunching through the grey slush snow that had refrozen overnight into brittle dirty sculptures. They gave way pleasingly beneath my boots.

The church was getting decked out in yellow and white and green, all colours that I recognised too as symbolically significant. Even the theme of rebirth and redemption was one that I shared with his faith. I decided I needed to chat to him sometime about Sian's plan and see if he could shed light on my unease.

It was a long slog up to the Tait's farm and when I arrived, only Mrs Tait was at home. She beckoned me in and I was delighted to see Seren lying in a jumble of old towels by the unlit

138

fire. She lifted her head and there was nearly a wag of a tail. I approached carefully and did a quick check of her. She had already put weight on, now she wasn't using all her spare calories just to stay warm.

Mrs Tait still didn't speak. She nodded, she smiled and she dipped her head from side to side, but not a word passed her lips. I established that Seren was doing just fine, and left them to it.

Because I had thought of Horatio, I then made my way with some purpose back down to his church.

***

I found him, not at home, but in the porch area of his church, sorting out the notices and posters that were on display there. He was staring at a sheet of paper that simply said, "For sale! Eighteen tennis balls. Used."

He looked up at me and brandished it in his pudgy hand. "But there's no contact details!"

"Did you want eighteen tennis balls?"

"I was tempted. They could be used at the Sunday School."

"Getting bored of pipe cleaners?"

"When a Sunday School teacher is bored of pipe cleaners they are bored of life and spiritually bankrupt too, I might add. Now, my dear, what is it that I can help you with?"

"How do you know this isn't a social call?" I said.

He raised one eyebrow. "The Lord works in mysterious ways. Also, you never come for any other reason. Come inside and let us sit down comfortably. Well, let us perch on a hard pew, anyway."

I liked the church for its peace and quiet. It was always peaceful, even on Sundays, as most people locally went to chapel rather than Church in Wales, if they attended any place of worship at all, which was becoming more rare. With that in mind, I told him about Sian Pederi's proposal.

He tapped his hands on the wooden back of the pew in front of him. "What an interesting idea."

"But do you think it's a good one?"

"For her to run these retreats, or for you to get involved?"

"Either. Both."

"What do you think?"

"I am not sure. I think it's dangerous. I think that you can't just meddle on the edges of magic, like some cosmic pick and mix."

He flared his nostrils. "I would agree and I would take it further and suggest that magic, or whatever it is, ought to be left very much alone. By everyone."

"Including me."

"Yes, of course."

"But you know that it would come looking for me anyway. The thing is, I never sought any of this out. But these people coming to a retreat will be seeking things out and they want to experience life-changing feelings and I'm just worried that it could go badly for them, especially with…"

There was a silence.

Horatio looked up at the vaulted ceiling, waiting for me to

finish what I hadn't realised I was going to say until I said it.

"...especially with Sian in charge."

"Has she power?"

"She has. I don't like it."

"Does she like yours? I don't."

He was honest and I loved him for it. "She doesn't like mine, no. I think she thinks it's inferior. Also I don't spend any money in her shop."

"So, in fact, she is intimidated by your power as you appear to need no props or crutches. Yet she came to you anyway."

"Just because I can be an attraction and make money for her."

"So cynical."

I was growing frustrated. But that was how Horatio sometimes worked. He'd let you talk on and on about things until you were talking about something else and that would turn out to be the nub of the matter.

I got to my feet.

"But Bron, the matter is not resolved."

"I know." I tidied up my woollen scarf and tucked my stray hair back under my hat, ready for the weather outside. "I've got some thinking to do."

"One thing, before you go," he said, hauling his bulk upright too. "Don't second guess her intentions. People have their own responsibilities and it's not down to you to interpret them."

"Er…"

He grabbed my wrist, and the church grew a few degrees colder, if that were possible. "You have told me more about yourself than her," he said, "dressed up as concern. Think on it. Go with God," he added blandly as he released me.

I shivered, and all I could say was, "Thanks. Wow, it's like a fridge in here."

He narrowed his eyes slightly and did not match my nervous laugh. "Blessings upon you."

"And on you."

I left. Fridge was *oergell* in Welsh – literally, cold-cell. A cell of cold. The prickling down my spine only gradually faded.

When I say that Horatio was sometimes paternal in his approach to me, that's not always a comfortable thing. Fathers chastise as much as they reassure, don't they?

For an hour I wandered, following no particular track, just letting myself be guided by the flash of a bird's wing or the rattle of a dry leaf in a bush. I trod old paths, and wondered idly if they were ley lines. Were they paths of power which attracted me to them, or had they become paths of power by the generations of magical feet that had walked them? It didn't matter. They just existed and that was enough.

My walking was an active meditation, reaffirming my connection with My Land, the source of my power, and I gave blessings where appropriate. The old stone at a crossroads received a wipe of spit from my finger, and a thorn bush had a flower carefully pinned to it – a crocus petal I had found, torn loose from its stem, abandoned and half-buried by snow. I gave some warmth to a blackbird who hid in the brown leaves of a beech hedge and I scattered some food from my pockets when I came to a place where I knew mice to be nesting.

And so, by roundabout ways, I came to the place that I had been intending to come for a little while now – the ramshackle shed that Dean, my druidic friend, called home. I hoped he'd be more reassuring than Horatio had been, though I wasn't ready to talk about Sian again today. I had another, very specific question for Dean.

From the outside, Dean's abode looked dire. It was an old prefab building, one of the blocky thin temporary accommodations that had been thrown up after the Second World War. It had been intended for use for only a few years. The corners were rotten and the roof appeared to be tied on with string. In a high wind, the walls shifted and bowed alarmingly. It stood on its own now, in the middle of a patch of scrubby land that no one could decide who owned. No one cared enough to push it. It was, and had always been, where the local druid lived.

Trees ringed the wasteland, and that was why he lived here.

Trees and songs and legend and lore were Dean's blood.

He was sitting on a stump outside his house, wrapped in a long dark coat, with a multi-coloured scarf layered around his neck with so many twists that it obscured the lower half of his face. He wore nerdish glasses that I didn't think he needed, but it added to his floppy-haired geeky charm. He reminded me very much of some actor I'd once seen that apparently played a new version of Sherlock, mixed up with all the different Doctor Whos there had ever been.

"*Shwmae, Bron, shwd wyt ti?*"

"I'm fine, thanks. You?"

"Pull up a stump," he said. "Or do you want to go inside?"

143

He looked wary, as well he might. The nature-is-everything theme did *not* continue inside Dean's house. I had peeped inside a few times, and he had hauled me away before my energies blew up one of his many computers.

It might have looked like a mad-hippy-in-the-woods place from the outside, but it was a veritable palace of tech on the inside. Almost entirely powered by renewable energy, too. You'd think that my energies would be fine with renewables, but no, I could blow up a solar-powered clock as easily as I could a regular one. Dean once tried to tell me about protons but my eyes had glazed over.

"Outside is fine," I told him, "I'm dressed for the weather."

We made chit-chat for a little while. He went inside and came out with a cup of tea for me, and something gingery and spicy for himself.

"Hey," I said, "You know songs and things, right?"

"A few hundred, yes. Any one song in particular?"

"I don't know. I want to see if you recognise this…"

"Oh no," he said in mock horror, raising his hands. "You're going to sing? Please, let me grab a harder drink than this first…"

"Hey! Cheeky sod. Please," I said. "This could be important." I told him first how the song had ended up in my head, and then I sang the snatches of lyrics that I had remembered.

"Oh," he said, suddenly very serious. "Here it is." He closed his eyes as he sorted through the vast catalogues in his mind.

He sang, "Pwca tamed by no man, no hand. Pwca pwca touches no land. Pwca run, pwca run, pwca fly."

He stopped and looked at me. "Shall I go on?"

144

"Is there harm if you do?"

"No, not at this moment, in the daylight."

I shivered. That sounded ominous. "Go on."

He wasn't singing much of a catchy tune. It was more of a three-note dirge. "Ware the eyes that see your soul. Ware the hooves that touch no soil. Fleet of foot and tear your soul. Through the air no soil no soil. No soul no soul. No soil no soil. No soul."

"That was horrible," I said when he finished. "I don't mean your singing. Was that the tune?"

"It was, as far as I know. And yes, it is not terribly tuneful. But this is not a song that is sung to entertain. It is a warning-song, one to learn from, not be amused by. It has to chill you to be effective."

"It's catchy but not in a good way," I said. "What does it mean? What is the lesson I should learn from it?"

"It's obvious, isn't it? Avoid the pwca!"

"I intend to. I've had some bad experiences with shapeshifting sorts."

"The pwca is a strange kind of shifter," he said. "You'll mostly see it as a horse, around here."

"That reminds me," I said. "What do you know of the Wild Hunt?"

"The Cŵn Annwn? Absolutely loads. But why? What do you want to know?"

"Did you know that Gruffydd shoes the horse of the King Arawn?"

"Of course he does."

Dean looked so unsurprised I might as well have been talking of a shopping list.

Then he began to ask me about Maddie, and once more I had to assure him that she wasn't really interested in dating right now, and he had to assure me that he wasn't hinting that he fancied her, no, not at all, but he was just being friendly. His face was quite pink and I charitably allowed myself to think it was simply the effect of his ginger tea.

***

Gruffydd and his connection had been troubling me and when I left Dean's place, I went up on to the forge. I had a particular question that I needed to ask the blacksmith. He was working hard when I entered the workshop, and I made myself a brew while I waited. He seemed to be engaged in a time-critical piece of metalworking. I was pretty sure I didn't want to distract a guy who was flinging basically molten lava around.

The first thing he said when he finished, and came over to where I was happily lounging, was, "Snow's coming."

"It's been snowing for days. I am so bored of snow, now. It was fun for, like, the first twenty-four hours."

"Yeah, it's pretty enough to look at, but a pain to have to go anywhere in it. I just want you to be ready for it, that's all."

I sat up. "Why?"

"Oh, don't panic! Just that you'll be needed a lot. People falling over, animals and old people and kids getting ill, they can't get out to the doctors or whatever."

146

"You make it sound like it's going to be really bad."

He held my gaze, and said, "It is."

I shivered. "Thanks. Yes, I'll get ready. When?"

He glanced over the workshop to where the door stood half-open. "Now."

I could not see anything through the door but a swirling whiteness. It didn't look like midday. It must have started in the past fifteen minutes, so I still had plenty of time to get home – after I'd asked him my question. I stood up.

"Gruffydd, one thing is bothering me."

"Lots of things are bothering you but you don't know how to ask," he said.

"I don't know what you mean. No, listen, stop teasing me. This guy, David Hudson, he fell and was injured badly enough that he died. So he must have fallen from a height."

"What, like a really big tree that happens to be out there on the hill that no one has noticed? That he was just climbing, for fun?"

"No, like he was dropped from a great height," I said, and I felt a little nervous about asking Gruffydd this, because there was an unpleasant little suspicion still in my mind about him. "So could the Wild Hunt have dropped him?"

He jerked his chin, and thinned his lips. "No, that isn't the sort of thing they do. They chase down evildoers."

"But could someone have got the Hunt to pick him up and then drop him?"

"How?"

I don't know, I wanted to wail. *You know this sort of stuff, not me.* "Well, maybe someone could have magically ordered the dogs or the horses, or the riders, to pick him up and then let him fall. That would be consistent with his injuries." *And with the fact that I've seen the Wild Hunt around, and I saw that strange magical spirit that I saw at the place of his accident*, I thought.

He laughed. "No one orders the Hunt to do anything except what the King himself commands. And no one orders *him* to do anything. He does as he always has done. *Long is the day and long is the night, and long is the waiting of Arawn.*"

"I've heard that before," I said. "What does it mean?"

"That is not up to me to say," he said. "I don't know." He grinned. "Maybe he just waits around a lot, you know?"

"You're a menace."

"And you are asking silly questions." He seemed taller and darker all of a sudden.

"I'm sorry. Should I be sorry?"

"For asking questions? No." Then he came closer to me and I could smell sweat and something else, something old. "But you should be careful. Go now, and collect your cousin on the way home, for I know she is in that shop and that shop is not the place to be, today." His voice boomed, echoing in my mind. "Go to your place of safety and take care. For you are not the only one asking questions, and some people are finding things out that they did not want to find out, and that will make them dangerous." It wasn't Gruffydd speaking now. This was prophecy.

This was *warning*.

I gulped but I would not be intimidated. Okay, so yes, I felt like I was going to pee myself but I would *never* show that. I could hear my voice wobble but I spoke anyway. "Uh, so, Gruffydd, do you know how Hudson died?"

He stepped back and he was normal again, just an everyday sexy blacksmith, smiling at me. "No, not a clue. Get you gone before the weather traps you here and I have to listen to your babbling for the next long day."

"Cheers, and love you too."

"Get out," he said happily, and returned to his work.

I stopped at the door. I had that horsehair thing of Chloe's with me, shoved in a plastic bag and buried in my ever-present backpack. I thought that I should ask him about it.

But when I looked back, he was hunched over a small anvil, tapping at something delicate with a hammer that looked ridiculously tiny.

"Go."

I went, and I was followed through the battering, freezing snow by a sense of deep unease.

FIFTEEN

I got to the town centre which was already emptying of people and traffic. When I entered the shop, I found Maddie was already getting ready to go home. Sian was looking worried, and she smiled with relief when I appeared. It was a genuine smile, too. I was surprised.

"Thank goodness," she said. "You two both better get home before it gets any worse. I'm closing for the day. I think most people are."

"Ahh, Bron, great timing! Sian was going to walk me home."

"How nice," I said, sounding way more sarcastic than I actually meant to. It was a really nice offer from Sian. "But then how were you going to get back here, Sian?" She lived above the shop.

She blinked. "Oh. I didn't think of that."

Maddie slapped her forehead dramatically. "Oh well, it doesn't matter now." She was well bundled up in clothing. "Let's go."

We trudged out. The road was eerily quiet, and the snow was already two inches thick underfoot. Visibility was down to a few dozen yards, if that.

I told her about my discoveries as we slogged our way through the weather. "Do you think Gruffydd could possibly be a suspect?" I asked.

"Oh my, what do you think?" Maddie said, a scornful and disbelieving note in her voice.

"No, I don't think so, at all," I said. "But what if my judgement is clouded because he's an old friend?"

"No. He's got the means to do it, sure, with his links to that Wild Hunt and all, but why? What would his motive be? On the other hand, you look at Chloe, she's got plenty of motive."

"But she seems so genuinely upset."

"Maybe she got Tait to do it for her. I mean, with what you said about the eldest kids marrying one another."

"Yeah but if you keep doing that, that's basically cousins marrying, and that doesn't end well."

"I don't know," she said. "I mean, it's worked for your royal family."

"Have you *seen* some of them? Way too many teeth. Still, I agree with you. Chloe is a huge suspect."

"Yet she is in our house," Maddie said. "Sorry, your house."

"You live there too. You can say that."

"You don't think I'm taking liberties?"

"No," I said, reassuringly. *But I can't help feeling that I am*, I added in my head.

We had to stop talking as the wind whipped up a fresh onslaught against us. We should have been home a lot more quickly but it was hard going. A tractor chugged past but that was all we saw on the roads.

We stamped our feet before falling at last into the utility room and disrobing.

I hadn't forgotten Chloe was still there, but it was a new shock all the same when we entered the kitchen and saw her. She was wearing yesterday's clothes – she hadn't brought more than a handbag with her – and she was sitting at the table, a half-full cup of coffee in front of her. She was staring blankly into the middle distance, and jumped with alarm when we came in, though surely she must have heard the outer door slam.

"Oh! That wind," she said, distractedly.

For a brief moment I wondered if she was some kind of weather-witch and had brought the storm down upon us.

No. I still couldn't detect any magic about her at all.

"The snow's pretty bad," I said. "How are you today?"

"Oh … I don't know. Fuzzy-headed." She launched into another set of thanks for letting her stay but I waved it away.

"It's fine, it's fine. You are welcome. Where's Dilys? Have you seen her yet today?"

"Yeah, she went out about an hour ago."

Maddie was halfway to the hallway but she stopped dead. So did I. I narrowed my eyes at Chloe. "It's blowing a hoolie out there. And she's not come back?"

"No, not yet."

"So where did she say she was going?"

Chloe didn't look like she'd slept a wink. She was drowsy, almost trance-like, but I could see her forcing herself to wake up. "Oh, god, I am so sorry, Bron. I didn't think. I can't

153

153

remember. She just got dressed in her outdoor stuff and went, you know? She didn't really say."

"*She didn't say* and *you don't remember* are two different things," I said.

"Bron, steady now," Maddie said, coming towards me, her arm out like she thought I was about to leap onto Chloe.

"She said, she said, she said she'd be home by one o'clock," Chloe said, and she looked anxiously towards the clock on the sideboard. "Oh I am so sorry! I have been feeling so … I can't sleep … oh. Oh, Bron." She was a woman deep in grief.

It was ten to one.

"She's never late," I said. "If she isn't back within ten minutes…"

"Then what?" Maddie said.

"Then I go to look for her."

We all glanced at the window where the snow was piling up in the corners of the frame.

"Shall I put the kettle on?" Chloe said, jumping to her feet, trying to be normal.

There was no point – if my aunt did not walk through that door very soon, I would be off and out into the storm once more – but I nodded, just to give her something to do.

We all nearly screamed when there was a hammering at the front door of the house.

The *front* door.

We never used it.

Maddie and I collided in the doorway to the hall, but I elbowed her out of the way and made it through first. Maddie shot to the window at the side of the big dark door and pressed her face to it, cupping her hands around to see more clearly. I dragged back the bolts and had to use both hands to turn the key in the lock. Any other time, I'd have gone out the back door and round the house to see who was there. But not today – not in this storm.

The door had an impressive squeak as I opened it, and snow swirled in. I didn't recognise the figure outside, save that he was tall, and male, and dressed in many dark layers of clothing.

"Is she here?"

Maddie threw herself against the door to close it against the man and I pushed too.

But he was already in, using his weight to grind it further open. "I mean no harm! Give me sanctuary, will you? Is she here? I know she's here."

I recognised that rough voice, the Welsh vowels long in his mouth; a hill farmer, a man unused to speaking English.

What did you say in such a situation? "No she's not" – who did he want, anyway? Or, perhaps safer, "There's just me and A TEAM OF REALLY BIG RUGBY PLAYERS and they just happen to be heavily armed."

Maddie spoke for me. "Who? Did you want to see Dilys?"

Edmund Tait pulled his balaclava from his head and stood panting heavily. "No, you know who I need to see. Chloe, isn't it! Shut the door, shall I?"

Maddie stared at me with frightened eyes. I took charge. After all, we could hardly shoehorn him out into the storm again, and I was stronger here in my own house. If he was in here, I could use more magic against him.

If I needed to.

I realised I was already assuming he was dangerous. *Honestly, just calm down*, I remonstrated with myself; *this is how miscarriages of justice happen. Don't assume the worst.*

He helped us to close the door and I bolted it again. But I didn't lead him into the kitchen. Chloe, I noticed, hadn't followed us into the dark and cold hallway. I guessed she would be listening, though.

"Hey," I said, trying to sound like this was a normal sort of thing. "I don't know you very well, and all that. But I have to ask. What are you doing out in this weather? Everyone is safer at home. You gave us quite a fright…"

He was not interested in my chit-chat. "I need to know that she's safe. Where is she?"

"Look, I can't just let you barge around in here. Sometimes people don't want to be found. Hey!"

He simply wasn't listening. He pushed his way past us, heading straight for the kitchen door as it was the only one that was slightly open, and the warm yellow light spilled out. "Chloe?"

"Hey, hey!" Both Maddie and I yelled at the same time, and we launched ourselves on him, grabbing an arm each. Harkin rose to the occasion too, and attached himself to Tait's calf, hanging on with his claws and teeth.

Tait began to jerk and flail as he tried to dislodge us all. I summoned every scrap of power that the house could give me and slammed it, hard, into his body. He staggered against the door frame but it trapped Maddie and she squealed and had to let go.

I had both my hands wrapped around his right arm and Harkin was still on his leg. I relaxed temporarily, and he regained his footing just long enough for me to gather another burst of energy. This time I used it to force him forwards the way he had already committed to going, and the unexpected shove from me sent him tumbling to his knees into the kitchen. There was an unpleasant crack of bone on the hard tiled floor.

"Wait, no, stop!"

Chloe's voice cut through us all.

Tait stayed on his knees. Harkin let go but remained poised by his leg. I had fallen to one side, and I crouched, my arms out in a defensive gesture. Maddie stood in the doorway, rubbing her arm.

We all stared at Chloe, who had tears running down her face.

"He is my friend. After everything. He is. Please, let him in."

SIXTEEN

Well, she might have said that he was her friend, but she didn't greet him in any kind of friendly way, unless living in London *really* changes a person.

Instead she stayed at the far end of the kitchen, and would not sit down. When he approached her, she moved away, flinching.

He put up his hands and stepped back from her, apologising in Welsh.

Maddie said, very brightly, "So, I'll put the kettle on, right?"

Every head swivelled towards her.

"Er, Maddie…?"

"Sorry," she said, in the most Californian accent I'd ever heard her utter. "I just thought that's what you people did in this kinda situation."

It temporarily broke the tension. "Yeah, go on, then," I said.

I turned my attention back to the curious tableau being played out between old-style hill-farmer Edmund Tait and his childhood friend, the now-cosmopolitan Chloe Davies.

Chloe looked at me.

Tait looked at Chloe.

She was not happy.

And then I looked at the clock and I saw that it was a quarter past one, and there was no sign of Great Aunt Dilys.

"Why did you come here?" I said, addressing both Chloe and Tait. I didn't want to be dealing with this right now. Fear made me brusque.

Tait said, "To find Chloe."

"How did you know she was here?"

"I asked around, and her mum said she might have come to see Dilys because she'd been before."

"And did you? Chloe, come to see Dilys?"

"I came for some space," she said, angrily. "I told you that yesterday. I meant it." She shot a venomous look at Tait.

"You are safer with me, not on your own," Tait said.

"Safe from *what?*" she spat out.

He didn't answer. Instead, he pulled out a chair and sat down. "Well, with the storm as it is, I suppose none of us are going anywhere." He finally looked at me. "I am sorry for bringing all this down on you. It isn't any of your business. You don't need to worry about it."

"As it happens, I have much more important things to worry about," I replied.

Maddie brought the teapot over and put it on the table. She started to lay out cups and milk and sugar, every inch the proper British role-model. She even fetched the tin of biscuits.

No one helped themselves to any of the things on offer.

"What about Dilys?" Maddie said.

160

"Yeah." I had mulled over the options in my head, and I came to a decision. "I am going out to find her."

"You can't!" Maddie said in horror. "I didn't mean that. You don't know where she went, and the weather, oh my, you'll die!"

"I reckon I can work out where she went," I said. I went out to the utility room where the animals were all still and silent in their cages, hiding under piles of straw and bedding until the storm had gone. I ran my eyes along the shelf. I knew exactly what herbal preparations I should see there – these were things I had recently made up to help the local people and the local animals.

There was a space, and it should have contained a jar of paste made from oak bark.

"She's gone to see Mrs Harrington," I said, going back into the kitchen, and in spite of the otherwise grave situation I will confess I felt a little smug. "Mrs Harrington has some mouth ulcers and I made that paste up yesterday."

"Ivy Harrington?" Tait said. "She lives a mile out east of here. You can't go there, the road's impassable."

"I can't drive, anyway," I said.

"No, go into town, to the police station and ask for help," Maddie said.

"For god's sake!" Chloe slammed her hands onto the table and made all the crockery rattle. "You're all idiots, the lot of you! Just phone up!"

Maddie stared at me, then looked away in embarrassment.

"The phone lines are all down," Tait said.

Chloe pulled her smart phone from her pocket. "Yeah but who uses landlines these days?"

Even Tait had heard of my issues with technology. But Chloe had been living away for years. She stared at her phone. "Something's wrong. I thought it was funny when I couldn't get online last night. Well, someone else can call Ivy Harrington and see if your aunt is there…"

"We can't," I said, feeling sick, like all of this was my fault. "None of you can use your phones because of me. I mean, I could go out into the garden maybe and shield myself and maybe the house will let you try, but it won't always work. I'm too embedded in this whole place."

"Don't talk nonsense. Someone, give me a phone…"

"It's true," Tait said. "You can feel the static around her."

He was wrong. It wasn't static – I don't walk around with my hair standing on end – but that made me pause. So he could detect my power, could he? He couldn't identify it but he knew it was there. He knew I was more than a healer.

"We are wasting time!" I shouted. "Maddie, you explain to them. I'm going to get Dilys. All of you, stay here."

"No, you can't–" Tait began.

I glared at him. "Don't make me set my cat on you again," I warned him. "Or worse." I stamped over to the utility room and started to layer on clothing. "It makes sense. As soon as I am clear of this place, you can maybe get your phones to work again. You might need to go into the garden. You can call the police. But I am going towards Ivy Harrington's house, because if I go to the police station, to be honest, do you think they will drop everything? I bet they are snowed under – haha, sorry, not funny – with other things to do. But if I stay, Dilys could be in trouble. And if someone else goes, no one here can call for help."

I was ready. I picked up my backpack, and grabbed a few biscuits from the tin, cramming them into my mouth. Then I stood in the doorway, and tightened the scarf around my face, still chewing. "Anyway," I said, as if it made everything all right, "I will have Harkin, and this is my land. Nothing really bad can happen to me here."

Harkin jumped up into my arms and I tucked him into my coat, tightening a belt around the outside so that my jacket billowed out to make him a secure and cosy nest against my chest.

Tait opened his mouth but he snapped it shut before he said anything.

Chloe and Maddie were looking at me in big-eyed horror.

Then Maddie gave me the smallest of nods, and I left before I could let good common sense catch up.

Seventeen

What if Edmund Tait was the murderer? It was on my mind as I plunged into the icy storm. We'd considered him as a strong suspect. And I was leaving Chloe and Maddie in the house with him? Was I leaving them in potential danger?

Don't second-guess someone's intentions, Horatio had said.

And anyway, what if my aunt was out here in the storm, and lost, or injured?

I hoped that I was going to find her cosily in Ivy Harrington's sitting room, drinking tea laced with brandy. I hoped against hope that I was going to look like a massive fool. I prayed to every deity I'd ever heard of that I was going to be mocked for my stupid dramatic overreaction.

Because public humiliation would not kill me.

The slim chance that my aunt could be caught in the storm on her way back, though – that was unbearable. I would never forgive myself if anything happened. She would have left Ivy's house before the storm clamped down, I thought, running through the timescale in my head. Dilys was always on time. She would have had to have left before the snows came.

The very best case scenario would be that she turned back to Ivy's house.

The other option would be that someone would have picked her up in their car – but she had not come home. If someone had picked her up, she would be back by now.

Harkin mewed and called to me, and he was distressed by something. I pushed a hand inside my coat to calm him. He licked my fingers. I called up as much power as I could, forming a warm sphere around us, just extending a few inches from my body. It wasn't much but it was enough to melt the snow before it landed on us. I didn't want to waste my powers, but nor did I want to die of frostbite.

Harkin grew more urgent with his message to me, and I knew, in a flash, that he meant Dilys; he was showing a quite different level of disquiet to his usual "come find this animal in need" behaviour.

I quickened my pace. I'd been acting on instinct, and my instinct was often right; I stopped trying to analyse and think and second-guess events. Now was simply the time to act.

I was lucky that here, there were houses on either side of the road. It sheltered us from the worst of the storm, but soon that shelter would run out. This road was one of the ways out of town, up into the hills. The next large settlement was seven miles away. There was still a footpath but I could have walked in the road as no vehicles were moving past. The only sound was the howling wind.

And screaming.

The screaming? Er, oh … *what?* I listened more closely. Was

166

it screaming laughter?

I pushed my hat a little higher. It kept falling down to obscure my eyes. Up ahead was a plastic bus shelter, closed in on all sides but for a small gap to let people in and out. I could see, now that I was close, a blur of dark figures standing inside the structure, and I could hear hysterical adolescent giggling.

I slammed myself up against the Perspex and made them all scream with genuine fright. Then I stuck my head through the gap. "Oh, hi, sorry about that. Did I startle you?"

Lacey had her hand over her mouth. "Oh my *god,* did you have to?"

"Yeah, I did. What are you lot doing out here in this? Don't you have homes to go to? There is a bit of weather happening, you know. You might have noticed."

Kelly and Eira were flanking their ringleader. Eira had a bottle of something bright pink in her hands, and I recognised a particularly vile cheap alcoholic drink.

They were all quite, quite tipsy.

"Why stay at home when we can be one! With! The! Stoooooorm!" Eira sang.

"Oh shut up," Lacey snapped at her. "What are *you* doing out here?"

I could see – and smell – that Lacey was not as drunk as the other two. "I am rescuing my aunt."

"That Dilys?"

"Yes. She's out there in the storm, trapped somewhere between here and Ivy Harrington's house. I have to get to her."

"How do you know she's trapped?"

Harkin mewed. I levelled my very best withering stare at Lacey. "I am a witch. Duh."

"Yeah, yeah, all right then, so magic her some help." She wriggled her gloved fingers in the air and made a woo-woo noise.

"I am using what magic I can. Have you noticed the snow falling on me?"

Lacey blinked. "Oh. It's … not." The visible display of power had more of an effect on her than any number of words could have done. More humbly, she said, "Right. Uh, so do you need help?"

I could have kissed her. "Actually, yeah. Can you guys run into town and alert Adam at the police station? Or anyone at the police station? Even Polly Jones will do." They wouldn't encounter as much of the storm by going that way. And I wanted them to get to real shelter because I just *knew* that things were going to get worse.

"And say what to the police? Are they going to believe us or what?"

"Tell them I have had to come out to find my aunt. Also, oh god, Maddie is at home with poor Chloe Davies and that Edmund Tait has turned up and I don't trust him one bit."

"At home? Your place?"

Harkin was struggling now, becoming frantic. "Yes. I have got to carry on," I said in a rush. "Tell them just what I said and get them to send someone out to here. Mention my name. I *know* my aunt is out there, I can feel something now … oh my god, she's definitely injured…" Panic rose within me as new sensations flooded my awareness.

168

"Go, go!" Lacey commanded, seeing my distress. "Right, don't worry. We're on it. I was bored out here anyway. Come on Eira, Kelly."

Eira was still singing, which was appropriate as her name meant "snow." Lacey towed them both out into the storm, and I continued on my way, as fast as I could, my feet slipping and sliding in the piling drifts.

Where the trees and walls to the side thinned out, the wind was coming in strong bursts now and would buffet me to and fro. I had no shelter at all. Visibility continued to reduce. I sent my awareness ahead but it was blocked by the storm and it made my concentration move away from the warm bubble I was trying to keep around me. Magic is infinite, of course, but my use of it was hampered by my own fragile mortal state. Or, in other words, you can't shove Niagara Falls into a baby's sippy cup.

Harkin began to squirm and squeal. I stopped to push my hand into my coat again, and he took the opportunity to claw his way free. I called him but the rising wind tore the words from my lips, and he disappeared into the snow.

I could not tell how far I was from Ivy Harrington's house. I could only just be sure that I was still on the road. Whiteness surrounded me.

And I was alone.

Eighteen

Something called to me in my head, an echoing sensation that dragged me forwards. It was Harkin and I felt relief – but almost instantly, that relief was replaced by more worry and concern. Harkin's call for help contained another's thought-call.

Great Aunt Dilys.

I could feel Dilys's presence wrapped up in Harkin's telepathic communication, as if my cat was relaying her desperate call for help.

That was why he had run off ahead.

The storm came at me in force now, and I started to wonder if there was more to this than simply "nature" – whatever *that* was. Of course nature contained magic. It was, in many cases, just science we hadn't explained yet. Electricity was magic, once.

Still that was no use to me, though. I had some hard decisions to face once all this was over.

But for now, I had to forge ahead. If Dilys was calling me through Harkin, it confirmed my intuition that something was wrong and that she needed me.

Wait, stop, hang on just one minute. I forced myself to stop and

I turned to present my back to the howling wind. *This is exactly how stupid heroines in silly novels get killed,* I reminded myself. I was the most sensible logical choice to leave the house, so they could use their phones to call for help. I had sent the teen gang into town too, for their own safety and to pass the word on. So far, I felt I had been as sensible as I could be, under the circumstances.

But it would do no one any good if I ended up dying of exposure out here. My magic was keeping me warm – but for how long could I sustain that?

Did I have any other options? I forced myself to think. I didn't want to win any Darwin Awards for most foolish decision and stupidest way to die.

Yes, I bloody well did have other options. I was not alone. I crouched down and began to centre myself, weaving a psychic circle around me, begging the quarters for protection and strength and wisdom.

I could not do this on my own, but I didn't have to. Harkin was with Dilys, and I knew she was alive, so that was something. I needed back-up. I hoped that Adam or one of his colleagues would be on their way to me, but I also knew they had many other emergencies to attend to.

There was magic in the grey-white air, magic in the biting wind, magic in the snow that hissed and melted two inches from my head. There had been no magic on Chloe, but Edmund Tait was from a family who reeked of the stuff.

Old magic.

And I knew who else could handle old magic – who might even be responsible for some of this, too.

Gruffydd.

He was the one that I needed to call. He was powerful and he knew about storms and the Wild Hunt and he was the one I felt could help me now.

I wasn't sure if I had enough of a connection to him, but we were old friends and pagan allies so that had to count for something, didn't it? And then I remembered Rhiannon.

I closed my eyes and called for her help. She was not a goddess that I often worked with, but she was a strong woman and she rode a horse – there had to be a way for her to help me contact Gruffydd. If I had to journey into myself and use the corpse roads, I would, but it would leave my body vulnerable out here in the open. I had to try a more sensible way first.

I suppose "sensible" is relative.

I'd looked up the stories of Arawn after my meeting with Dean. Rhiannon was married to Pwyll once; and it was Pwyll's hounds that drove away the Cŵn Annwn, King Arawn's own dogs, from a wounded stag and brought a curse down upon himself that he lifted when he defeated Hafgan, a rival king.

And she was a powerful queen.

I called her through appealing to her three birds, the ones that call the dead to wake and the living to sleep, I called her through her white horse which she rode so slowly, so majestically, I called her by her strength and her wisdom.

I called her as a Daughter of Wales, *Merch o Gymru*.

Something rocked me, and lifted me off my heels slightly, and it was not the wind. I remembered that she would carry travellers on her back and I realised that it was her presence. I couldn't form the words I needed to tell her why I'd called her, not in English nor in Welsh. But I could conjure up an image of Gruffydd in my mind, painting it with as much detail as possible. I drew in the forge around him, and the feeling of him, the scent of him, the purpose of him.

Another jolt rocked me, like an earthquake no one else could detect, and then it vanished.

But there was a fine thread of silver, only visible to my mind's eye, which spooled out from my own heart and disappeared into the snow and wind behind me. I could feel it rushing away while the end stayed firmly connected to me.

I could not imagine what that meant, exactly, but I took comfort from it. I got to my feet, and leaned forward into the wind, and began to make my way forwards into the ever-increasing storm, intent now on getting to Dilys and Harkin, and trusting to the goddess that she would bring Gruffydd to me.

I tried not to think of Maddie and Tait and Chloe in the house together. I didn't trust Tait and I wasn't sure I trusted Chloe, altogether. And Chloe was scared of Tait, which worried me. Maddie was growing more powerful and capable, but would it be enough? She was on her home turf, such as it was, in the house – but Tait was in his own *land* and I wondered if that was a stronger thing.

And if my suspicions were correct and Tait was somehow – but how? – responsible for David Hudson's death, then had I put them all in more danger?

I could *not* allow myself to get distracted. I had to trust to Maddie, and focus on my own problems right now. My magic was faltering. Snow was beginning to land on me. I could draw on as much energy as I needed, but I was losing the ability to control it fully. And you never, ever want to deal with magic when you're tired. That's how people end up asleep for a hundred years under a bush, or selling their soul at crossroads, or getting into dodgy musical competitions with suave and smooth-tongued horned demons.

There always has to be a balance. Everyone knows this. I could not take-take-take.

But I *had* to – just for a little longer.

I'd pay for it later.

I wiped the snow from my face and grunted, and whimpered, stumbling as my feet sank up to the ankles in the snow now. *Onwards,* I told myself. The thread that spooled out from me began to tug and pull.

Something loomed up at my side and I fell away from it, my heart leaping into my mouth. I scrabbled on my knees, my hands raised up, the snow blinding me. Suddenly there was a blue flash, a silent expansion from the space between me and whatever the big dark shape was, and the storm was around us – but not touching us. We were in a safe bubble.

We?

Me and Gruffydd, but this was not the blacksmith as I knew him. For one, he was astride a huge grey horse, slate-grey, with old eyes like that of an elderly druid I'd once met. He rode with no saddle and, strangely, no bridle either, and the horse skittered like it was going to rear up. I braced myself. But Gruffydd had perfect control.

He wore a battered green waxed jacket and long brown leather boots, and was bare-headed in spite of the weather. But his control of the storm made my own efforts look paltry and embarrassing.

This man *owned* it.

He looked down at me, his face grim, suddenly looking twenty years older than he really was.

He looked fell. I don't think I've ever seen anyone for real looking "fell" – it was just a word from fantasy novels up until this point.

But Gruffydd was now the default image in my mental dictionary. Also filed under "severe," "imposing", and "frankly terrifying."

He leaned down and I had to fight the urge to actually cower away from him.

He grabbed my arm, and something shifted, for the next thing I knew, I was sitting behind him, on the back of the horse, and I nearly fainted with the dizzying sensation.

"Where?" he demanded.

I realised he was using a hell of a lot of his own power right now, and talking in full sentences was not top of his list of priorities.

"Forwards towards Ivy Harrington's," I said. "Dilys is–"

"Got it. I know. Hold on."

Nineteen

I had never ridden a horse in my life before.

I wasn't entirely sure that this even counted as "riding." More like "clinging on out of sheer terror" perhaps. Gruffydd's power held the worst of the storm off us all, and I was able to let down my guard a little, and recharge as much as I could. The horse's spine was unexpectedly uncomfortable and I shifted my position but it wasn't the easiest ride. Now I knew why people used saddles. The horse was also wider than I had imagined. By moving myself backwards rather than pressing against Gruffydd I was able to avoid some of the spine-and-width issues. But then I had less of a secure grip on his waist.

And I had to concentrate on finding Dilys. The silver thread had gone now; it must have been something Rhiannon had cast, and I made a mental note to perform some rituals especially for her. I wasn't a great ritual person but it was only right, in this case.

So I cast my awareness forwards and when I latched onto Harkin's plaintive call, I urged Gruffydd on. "We're nearly there … keep going … but to the left," I yelled.

The horse was thundering along in a rocking motion – I think that might have been a canter. Suddenly we heard very faint, quavering yelling, and the horse slowed, now trotting forward in a jerking, bouncing movement and I was flung once more against Gruffydd's back, every step knocking the wind out of me.

"Hello!"

"That's Dilys," I shouted. "Hello! Hello!"

There was no reply. She must have been saving her energy for when she heard us approach, but that had been too much for her.

Gruffydd said, "Get off," and I did the most inelegant and ungainly dismount possible, landing in a crumpled heap way too close to the horse's dancing hooves. Gruffydd seemed to merely twitch his legs and there he was, landing lightly on his heels, and looking down at me with a pitying expression.

But there was no time to engage in mocking. He raised his hand to extend the blue sphere around us, and the storm withdrew, but it felt almost resentful about it.

There she was. Just a pile of clothes, topped by white snow, like rubbish abandoned twenty feet away up a hill. I ran and Harkin leaped at me, greeting me with purrs and yowls.

I pushed him away. "Dilys? Dilys?" Her skin was chilly under my hands.

How on earth had she ended up here, not on the road?

"You silly old woman," I muttered.

Her eyes fluttered. "Not as silly as you," she whispered. "What are you doing out in this?" Her voice was just a breath.

"Just, you know, rescuing you like a goddamn hero," I said, affecting Maddie's accent but in a bad way. "What's happened?"

"My ankle," she said. "I can't…" She wheezed, and I laid my hands on her shoulders, exerting a light but firm pressure.

"Hush, then don't talk. Let me do my thing."

Gruffydd came up behind me and he knew that this was my area of expertise now. He provided light, and shelter, and a blast of energy that rocketed right through me and made my hair stand on end and my stomach turn to liquid.

Dilys sagged back. I could see she was exhausted and freezing, so the first thing I needed to do was give her warmth and energy. I kept my hands on her, and let the power trickle slowly from me to her, not wanting to overwhelm her system. Harkin pressed against her, too. Gruffydd put his hands on my shoulders and together we got Dilys warm. As Gruffydd put his smelly coat over her, I moved down to her ankles, and I could immediately see what the problem was – no limb should rest at that sort of angle.

I had dealt with this kind of thing, and much worse, over the years. I've never really understood that thing that says women can't stand the sight of blood. I mean, we see the stuff, and worse, every month, for a start. I've also delivered babies, both human and animal. I've seen leg bones sticking out of skin and abscesses and sores and things that I am not even going to list here. You know exactly what I mean.

But this was my own aunt, and it made it very hard to deal with dispassionately. I had to steel myself to see her as no more than anonymous meat, just flesh and blood, as I hovered my hands above her ankle.

It was not broken. I don't know how she'd managed to twist it so badly, and why it looked so wrong; then I searched further and realised that her Achilles' tendon had ruptured. The pain must be intense, I thought, and this was not as easy as a straightforward break.

She needed urgent medical help.

I did not touch her ankle but I now began to flood her with as much relaxation as I could, doing anything I could to wrap her up away from the pain. She breathed out loudly and her eyes were closed but her lids fluttered.

"Well?" Gruffydd said.

"She's snapped a tendon in her ankle. At least. Maybe more injuries, and certainly hypothermia. She – what's that? Listen."

Harkin yowled. He had heard it too, and he ran down the banking towards the whited-out road.

Through gaps in the whirling snow, I could see a large four-wheel-drive vehicle churning its way along, snow chains rattling. It was liveried up with the mountain rescue badges all over it, and someone was hanging out of the passenger window, yelling. A strong light bounced off the swirling snowflakes.

Gruffydd yelled back and slithered down to greet them, leaving me with Dilys and – I realised – the horse which was standing still and simply staring at me in a very unsettling way. Horses didn't look quite right when you considered them head-on. I shivered.

But I wasn't going to try to shoo it away.

When Adam appeared at my side, I didn't waste time with

floods of tears or effusions of relief. He passed me a pen and told me what time it was, which I wrote on her forehead while he got organised with the two other mountain rescue guys behind him. They unravelled the straps from a bright orange plastic stretcher.

And then I was eased to one side after telling them all her name and approximate age, and no she had no health problems, and yes she was conscious, and no we had not moved her, and no we had not given her anything, and yes her ankle was just like that when we found her, and it was clearly a snapped tendon, and…

"I'll stop you there, then," the more beardy of the two rescue men said. "That's up to the hospital. We'll just get her there in one piece. Nye, you ready to lift? On my count."

I took another few steps back. The four men – Adam and Gruffydd included – lifted my poor fragile aunt as easily as if she had been a ragdoll and dropped her carefully onto the stretcher. Then the two mountain rescue men slid her down the slope.

Adam came to my side.

"Did you just happening to be out here, wandering in the storm?" he asked as we watched the men load her into the back of the all-terrain vehicle.

"No. I knew she was in trouble. But, Adam, there's other things going on."

"Tell me about it!" he groaned. "Power's out, comms are all down, there's broken legs every other street, missing pets, elderly folk with no heat, sick kids … it's a nightmare."

"No," I said. "Well, yes, all that. But I have to tell you that

I am *sure* that Edmund Tait had something to do with Hudson's murder."

"If it was murder."

"You know that it was!" I said as we started down the snowy banking to the road. "We just need proof. The only problem is, Tait is at our house right now. With Chloe. And Maddie."

Adam stopped and stared at me. "What?"

"Yeah, it's a mess," I said. "Chloe came to us last night, saying she needed a break, which I almost understood. Then Tait turned up this morning."

"Are they in it together?"

"I don't know. She didn't seem happy to see him. I didn't get a 'teamwork' vibe off them."

"Is she in danger, do you think?"

I felt a glow that this clever policeman was asking for my opinion. "I am not sure," I said truthfully. "Perhaps. Tait's impossible to read. He wasn't making threats. Maddie's there, at least."

"So she's in danger, too," Adam said.

"Maybe, but she's … strong."

"Is she a witch like you?" He was walking towards the waiting vehicle now. One of the mountain rescue men looked surprised but he turned away. What he didn't hear wouldn't harm him – that was a usual response in our small town.

"Not like me, but yes," I answered shortly. "She is."

"Right. Okay, you need to squeeze in, and shield up, and I'll get the lads to drop me and you at your house and they'll take Dilys up to the hospital … wow, did you ride here?"

Gruffydd had mounted his horse again and he was standing by the vehicle, smiling. The horse stood relaxed. Still none of the falling snow landed on either of them. My protection had given out for the moment – I had too many other things to deal with – and my hat was caked with snow.

"I did," Gruffydd said. "This is the original four-wheel-drive. Four-leg-drive, perhaps. Don't you worry about me. I'll sort myself out. Get her to safety."

He could have meant me, or Dilys. It didn't matter. I only noticed as he turned the horse away that he was now wearing nothing but a fisherman-style jumper, all hairy and ragged. His coat was still covering Dilys.

I was about to call out "wait" when he suddenly stopped anyway, and the horse's haunches bunched as it danced backwards, towards us. I drew away from it. The thing was *huge*.

Adam put out a hand to steady me and then we noticed what had made Gruffydd stop urging his horse on.

Three small figures were battling their way up the road, and one of them was waving a bottle, and singing a rude song about pirates.

TWENTY

"What on earth is this?" Adam said.

The beardy mountain rescue man popped his head out of the driver's side window. "Are you all getting in, or what?"

"Yes, we are, but let me just see what's going on here," Adam said. "Hey!"

Lacey, Eira and Kelly stumbled up to us. "You left us behind!" Lacey said.

"Yes, in a nice warm place out of the storm, you colossal idiots," Adam snapped. "We don't have the time or resources to deal with people who deliberately put themselves in danger. That's just plain irresponsible. Nye, do we have room for all this lot?"

Beardy-man scrunched up his face. "Not the horse as well, no."

"I'm riding home," Gruffydd said. "Don't mind me, like."

"No, wait, listen," Lacey said. "We left the police station because of what Bron told us about Maddie and that Edmund and Chloe. So we thought, we can be useful, and all that. You know, responsible. So we went to Bron's house, actually."

"And now I'm taking you home." Adam was getting angry. I hadn't seen him riled before, but he had good reason right now.

Still, I said, "Lacey, what was happening at my house?"

"Nothing. Except that only Maddie was there. Edmund took Chloe somewhere."

"Where?"

Lacey shrugged. "I dunno. Something wasn't right."

"Right, I'll ride on ahead, and see," Gruffydd said, and he kicked his horse forwards before anyone could say any different.

And the rest of us got piled into the mountain rescue Land Rover, crammed in the back and along the front seat too. I hunkered next to Dilys and held her hand. Adam was there with me, and Lacey and Eira. Kelly was shoved in the front in between the two mountain rescue men. I heard a mew, and knew that Harkin had secreted himself somewhere.

The vehicle was turned around by slow degrees and we began to make a bumping journey back into town. We'd pass our house on the way. I was going to let them take Dilys on to the hospital without me.

"I'm sorry," I whispered, and squeezed her hand.

She didn't speak. But I knew, that she knew, that I had to do this. She knew what I was going to do – probably better than I did myself.

TWENTY-ONE

No one spoke as we rocked from side to side. When the rocking stopped, I looked up and met Adam's eyes. He nodded slightly, and popped the rear door open. Lacey and Eira fell out into the snow, and Kelly climbed out from the front seat, clambering other men like a giggling spider. Adam got out with me, and slapped the bonnet so that the vehicle took off again. I watched it go. The snow still fell, in hard straight lines, but there was no wind at all.

"She will be fine," Adam said. "Don't look so worried."

"No … Harkin's still in there."

"Oh."

He would find his way home. Maybe he'd deliberately stayed with my aunt, anyway. Too much was happening at once, right now – before I could say anything else, Gruffydd emerged from the side of the house.

"Where's your horse?" Lacey asked.

"Out the back," he said. "Don't worry about that. Bron…"

"What? Where's Maddie?"

He looked even grimmer than he had earlier. Still the snow

didn't land on him. "I don't know. The back door was standing open, and the house is empty. Even…"

"Tell me!" I began to run past him but he caught hold of my arm and made me swing to a stop against him.

"All your cages are open. There's nothing in your house. Nothing at all. And no protection. It is as if your whole *house* is gone."

I understood completely. And the implications terrified me. If the spirit of the house had gone, what then?

"Are you sure?" I asked, stupidly.

"Let's get inside," Adam said. He came to the other side of me and with Gruffydd on one arm and Adam on the other, they led me into the kitchen. It was cold and dark.

"God, don't you even have heating?" Lacey said, prowling around and showing a distinct lack of shame regarding her nosiness. She prodded at a pile of magazines on the table which slithered out into a fan shape. I spotted a glove that I had thought I'd lost in town, and an unfamiliar shiny black rectangle that looked like a darker version of Maddie's iPad.

"I'm cold," Lacey was whining.

"The range is out. The range *never* goes out," I said. "I can't offer anyone a cup of tea…" Somehow it seemed vitally important that I make hot drinks for everyone.

"Hah!" Eira said. Her intoxication seemed to be wearing off, because she went to the range and unhooked one of the doors. "Yeah, just like my nan's. Right, I'm gonna need newspaper twisted up and some kindling and some matches."

Lacey and Kelly went to her aid.

Adam flicked a switch by the door but nothing happened. "I didn't expect the power to be on," he remarked. "Right, we need to search the house."

"There's no one here," Gruffydd said.

"If something happened – like a fight – someone might be hiding," Adam said.

"No," Gruffydd said, dropping his voice. "Trust me. There is no one here."

"He's right," I said. "I'd know. I'd *know*. This house is completely empty." I felt bereft, like I'd experienced a sudden and shocking bereavement. No spirits, no protection, not even the Tylwyth Teg.

Who I hadn't been feeding.

"We're here!" Lacey shrilled.

"It's empty," I repeated and when I looked at Gruffydd he nodded back at me.

Adam looked from me to Gruffydd and back to me. He struggled with his policeman-nature battling against his trust and understanding for me and my talents.

"Okay," he said at last. "So what do we think? Has Tait *taken* Chloe, or has she simply left with him?"

"He must have taken her," I said. "Something strange has happened, because if they had left of their own accord, Maddie would still be here."

"She was here when we came," Lacey pointed out. She half-closed her eyes as she sought to remember. "Let me think. Eira was singing something stupid so I didn't pay attention to what she said, exactly."

Suddenly Kelly came up to us. She stood in front of me, staring at the floor, and began to whisper something. I bent my head. I had never heard her speak before.

"Maddie was putting her boots on, so she must have been planning on leaving. She said, um, 'Did you see Bron? What are you even doing here? I've gotta go, he's gone away with her...'"

Even though her voice was low, her imitation of Maddie's accent and speech pattern was convincing. I believed her, and I felt she was giving me Maddie's words verbatim.

"And then she left?" I said.

Kelly nodded.

I turned to Adam. "They are all in trouble," I said. "I don't know what's happening but we have to find Maddie, and Chloe. And Tait. He *is* the murderer. I am sure of that now."

When I said that out loud, the three teenage girls hissed and gasped.

"You need a gun!" Lacey said, eyes wide. "Or knives or something. Do you have a shotgun?"

"Er, no, I'm more about saving lives," I said. "Anyway, you know, I do have magic."

"Has magic ever stopped a bullet?"

Adam stepped in. "You watch too much television, Lacey. I agree, Bron, we need to get out there. But..."

"I know. Don't worry. I understand and I will stay here," Gruffydd said.

"We need you!" I said.

He shook his head. "And if Tait comes back? Look, Eira's got the fire going now. We'll settle down, have a nice brew, and

190

I'm here in case anything happens. Where do you keep your biscuits?"

"The red tin is out on the table. Don't eat all the custard creams. Get that blue tin, too. There's a fruit cake in it."

Adam was at the door and looking back at me, his face set with lines I had not seen before. "Come on."

My mind was whirling. I forced myself to take a breath, then I grabbed a bit of fruit cake from Gruffydd's hands, and followed Adam out into the falling snow. He pulled his radio free from the pouch on his chest as we rounded the side of the house, and began to call the station.

By now, the snow was halfway up my shins. I had never known a storm like this at Eastertime before. Yes, we had late spring snows, far more often than we had snow before Christmas, but this was an unprecedented amount. I wondered if it was the same all over the country, and even all over Britain, but then I heard Adam's voice rise in annoyance.

"No, but Pol … no, yes, I understand that, but … there is a very strong chance that Edmund Tait is involved, somehow, in the death of David Hudson. Yes, but …"

Then he was silent, his frown deepening. I could hear his sergeant, Polly Jones, squawking through the radio but he had it held quite close to his head and I couldn't make out the words.

Then he pressed a button and shoved the radio back in its holster with a sigh.

"We're on our own."

"What did she say?"

We began to walk to the front of the house. "She's snowed

under – ha, ha, we've made that joke every half an hour now – with incidents and can't spare anyone for this wild goose chase."

Wild goose. I shivered. The calling of the geese, so like the Wild Hunt.

"What's up?" he said.

"Nothing." Then I spotted where the snow was flattened. The mountain rescue Land Rover had churned up a spot in front of the house, and its tyres tracks were still visible as deeper indentations in the snow, but alongside them I could see footprints. They were already fading, and indistinct, criss-crossing and overlapping so it was hard to tell how many people they belonged to.

But, crucially, they were the *only* footprints, and therefore, our only real lead.

I pointed, and together we began to follow them.

"Pol also said that I was stupid to be thinking of Tait. She reminded me that Hudson died by misadventure," he said as we stumbled along.

"We both know that isn't true."

"And she said that who Chloe chooses to go with is her own business as a grown woman."

"But it looks like Tait forced her."

"But did he? Really? I don't have the history here like you lot do. Pol pointed out that Chloe and this Tait are lifelong friends, and that everyone used to joke that they were destined to marry one another."

I nearly choked, but I kept walking. The prints were leading us along a side road that skirted the town centre. "Adam, that's it!" I said, trying to speed up.

"What, they've gone off to get married?"

"No," I said. "He's taken her for something like that, but it's definitely against her will. He's old-school and he believes the family myth. The myth that says the first born of his family marries the first born of hers."

"But, eww, cousins…"

"I know, I know," I said. "Explains a lot about his family."

"Ouch."

"Have you met them?"

"Yes … indeed."

"So you see," I went on. "Tait is utterly convinced that Chloe is his. It has been foretold. It is destined. She doesn't get a say in it. That's why he's killed her partner. And I don't think she would have known what Tait did, not at first. So she went to him, as a friend, for comfort. But unfortunately …"

"Oh my god. Yes," Adam said. "If you're right, then she's gone to him and he's thought hooray, she's mine…"

"And maybe he told her what he's done, and that's really why she came to us, for shelter while she worked out what to do."

I felt sad. She should have told me, somehow. We'd let her down. We hadn't provided any kind of shelter and now she'd been taken by this madman.

But where?

We put our heads down and followed the tracks.

The town was left behind us.

TWENTY-TWO

But as we walked, following the prints, we found that our progress circled around. Now the town was on our left and it seemed that we were heading back, eventually, to come out near the sports centre.

I stopped. "Wait. Are these footprints even real?"

Adam grabbed my arm. "Of course they are. What do you think made them? A dog wearing shoes out for a stroll?"

I wrenched my arm free. "Listen, we're hungry, tired and stressed. Take a moment. We're dealing with magical things here, and the thing is, magic isn't so black and white. It isn't a matter of good and evil. There are grey areas, and tricks, and illusions. It's called glamour. Maddie is a source of glamour, but she's new to it all, and she's easily fooled herself. We can't afford to jump onto the most visible, easiest clue. Close your eyes. Now, where do you *think* Tait might have taken Chloe?"

Adam half-closed his eyes but I saw a shine between the lids. And he shook his head. "I don't know. A registry office in Dolgellau?"

"Dolgell-*ee*," I corrected him but without malice.

"Did I get the double-l right?"

"No, but that's too big of an ask right now," I said. "Okay, he will have gone somewhere special and somewhere powerful. So definitely not Dolgellau. I think it's pretty obvious."

"Is it?"

"The stone circle by the Tait's farm."

"There's no stone circle up there," Adam said.

"There is, and we found it," I said.

"Can you find it again? In the snow? With the light fading?"

I wished Maddie was right with me. She could have followed a ley line right to the place. But I plastered on a fake smile. "Of course!" I said. "It's in a field with three hawthorns. Anyway, magic, right?"

"Right."

He looked like he believed me and I had to live up to his expectations now.

I couldn't let anyone down.

The consequences could be death.

Or worse.

***

Adam hesitated before following me away from the footprints. They'd become too obvious, too regular, too clear – that just confirmed to me that they were fake. It might not be the Faeries working against us, but it was a trick all the same.

At first, it was easy to find the way. We both knew where the Tait's farm was, and in spite of the falling snow, we could follow the whited-out road because of the stone walls and fences alongside.

Gradually the snowfall began to ease. Now it was swirling and dancing, but we could see further ahead, and in a funny way it disorientated me. Everything around us was white.

"We should be wearing sunglasses," Adam said. "We're going to get snow blindness."

"Is that even a thing?" I said.

"Yes, but the pain won't kick in until later, so we've got a window of opportunity before the damage really stops us."

"Oh, great." I slitted my eyes, but I knew it wasn't going to help much.

"Is that a farmhouse up ahead?" Adam said.

"It might be."

But it wasn't, it was just a barn, and I realised that I had missed the track we were supposed to be on. I spun around, searching through the endless glare for anything that could orientate us.

Adam pulled out his mobile phone. "Step away," he said.

"I thought all comms were down."

"They are, but I downloaded loads of maps onto here a few months ago, back when Dean and I were planning our camping trips. I will still be able to connect to the GPS, even if data is unavailable."

He could have been speaking Icelandic for all I could understand of that. I nodded. "Oh, right."

He half-smiled, and he knew I didn't have a clue. I stepped back and continued to look around.

"Is this stone circle marked on the Ordnance Survey maps?" he called over to me.

"No, I don't think so. But it's where seven ley lines converge."

Even at the distance of ten metres, I could hear his exasperated sigh. "And are ley lines, whatever they are, marked on the maps?"

"Not exactly," I said. "But we can use a map to find a possible line. I don't suppose you have a paper map on you, do you?"

He rolled his eyes.

"Right, okay, so that's a no," I said. I sighed. "Modern life really is awkward. Okay, what you're looking for is a series of sacred sites that all line up. Really old churches, you know, the ones with circular walls. Holy wells, stone circles, tumuli, barrows, um … anything, you know, old. Pagan. Oh, old fords, and old tracks, the sorts of tracks that have been worn really deep into the ground. And summits."

"For goodness' sake," he said, pinching his fingers on the screen, and swirling the display around. "Surely, mathematically speaking, you can make any line from those things?"

"Perhaps," I said. "But they feel different, too, when you walk along them."

"Are you sure this isn't your mind playing tricks because it's what you expect to feel?"

"Do we have time to argue?"

He grunted in response and continued to stab his finger at his phone.

Then he said, "Okay, so if we assume the track to the Tait's farm is one, and there's another line here that starts at the church, and goes through a well and a ford … and another perhaps coming from the top … well, there's three and maybe, just maybe, I can find the place where they all intersect." He looked up and down a few times. "I can't find seven. I am not totally sure about these three. My phone's display isn't exactly optimised for ley lines. Maybe that's a gap in the market for some mystical app. Okay. I'm still getting my head around this but I *think* I've plugged in the coordinates correctly. It should lead us to it. Let's go."

There was no snow falling at all now, but the sky above us remained leaden-grey and the air was bitingly cold. I was glad I'd eaten those few biscuits and cake but my stomach was rumbling. Adam was following the mobile phone's instructions and I couldn't walk too close to him, for fear of knocking the phone out of action.

So it was a strange and oddly lonely walk-half-run that we did, ploughing on up the hillside, trusting to Adam's map reading and his untutored interpretation of the symbols.

I sent out my senses, trying to feel for any ley lines, or whether I could detect Maddie calling for help, or any disturbance of power that would signal the whereabouts of Edmund Tait, but it was as if the snow had blanketed everything in a mystical sense as well as a physical one.

Something *was* out there, but not in the direction we were going. I called to Adam to stop for a moment. He turned, and it was as if he was seeing me for the first time.

"Are you all right? Oh my god, we've been walking for ages, and before that you were in the snow with your aunt…"

"Do I look that bad?"

"You look almost blue. Wait." He fished around in his pocket and pulled out a small silver packet. He threw it to me and I fumbled the catch, letting it thud into the snow.

"Sorry! My hands are cold. What is it?"

"An energy gel. Get that down your neck," he ordered.

I usually hated the things but I was grateful for this blast of sugar and electrolytes. I rolled the packet up to squeeze out the very last drop. He was swallowing one himself, I noticed.

"Thank you," I said. "But that's not why I stopped you. Are we definitely going in the right direction?"

"Yes, according to the map and my dodgy calculations," he said.

"Well, something over that way is calling to me," I said, pointing away from us, where there was a fence, a gate and a snow-covered tree.

Suddenly something moved. At first I thought it was a bird like a black crow landing on the fence, but it emerged into the gap made by the open gate, and I saw that it was a figure.

"Maddie!" I screamed and ran towards her. Then I stopped. Was it my cousin or was it another illusion to throw us off the scent?

"Bron!" she yelled back, and I ran forward again. We collided in the snow, hugging and celebrating and searching one another's faces for signs of injury … or enchantment.

Adam came up but hovered a little way away. Maddie

beckoned him forwards but he waved his phone at us, and nodded at me.

Ouch. I put my hands in the air, and backed away myself. "Maddie, go and see if he's on the right lines. Well, the right ley lines ... we have to get to the stone circle."

"We're not far," said Maddie and pointed the way we had been going.

"Then what were you doing?" I asked, suddenly suspicious. "You weren't heading in the right direction."

She glared at me, and her cheeks went pink. "I needed to pee."

"So you went off over there behind a tree?" I couldn't help it. I started to laugh. "Who were you hiding from?"

"It's just what you do, right."

Adam, too, was chuckling. Maddie huffed. "Don't we have a job to do?"

Instantly, we were all serious again.

"Yes," I said, and turned to face up the blank white hill. "And we need to move quickly…"

"And silently," Adam said. "I don't want to startle Tait into doing something … rash."

We all felt a lot, lot colder.

Twenty-three

The endless whiteness surrounded us. The snow had completely stopped now. Our feet broke the crisp crust and sank deeply into the thick snow that blanketed everything. It made our progress slow, and unexpectedly loud. It turns out that you cannot walk silently through snow.

But we tried, following in one another's footsteps to minimise the sounds of crunching. In places, the snow was so deep that you couldn't see the tops of the walls, because the driving wind had piled the snow up in banks against the stones, and it just looked like an undulating patch of ground. The lack of field boundaries was disconcerting. Still the sky was grey, and it cast a shimmering pallor over the otherwise dazzling white.

Adam was ahead of us, and he raised his arm to make us stop. We came up to his side.

He pointed. "There."

Yes. I could see them now. And I realised that even though the stones were hidden, the power in the place was not, and that was the important thing. I saw the tall, rangy form of Tait as he walked a slow circle widdershins. And in the centre was another figure, just standing, her arms by her sides and her head hanging down.

Chloe.

Was she there by choice or by enchantment?

Who would choose to stand in a field of snow with a madman and a potential murderer?

"Now what?" I whispered.

"Radio for back-up," Maddie said, elbowing Adam.

"I've tried that," he said. "And back-up for what, exactly? There's no crime in standing in a field. They are both currently innocent. We're the dodgy ones."

"Let's get closer."

We moved, trying to use bushes for cover. We were side by side now, not following in one another's footsteps. Tait looked absorbed in his task. I covered us in as much protection as I could. I could not make us invisible but I could weave a kind of deflection around us. It would lose effectiveness the closer that we got, and it was hard work. I was already drained.

The air still seemed to shift around us, like when you catch movement out of the corner of your eye in a mirror. I turned around and looked back the way we had come.

"Oh, hey, guys, hang on a minute," I said quietly.

They turned. "What now? Are we being followed?"

"No. In fact, no one could follow us. We aren't leaving any footprints anymore."

"What does that mean?" Adam said.

"We're between the worlds," I said. "Normal rules no longer apply."

"What rules do apply, then?" I could hear a waver in Adam's voice. This was far, far out of his usual comfort zone.

"Expect the unexpected."

"That is not helpful."

"I'm sorry. Whatever happens now, you have to trust me."

"Us," said Maddie.

I swallowed. I did trust her, but not the Tylwyth Teg. Now, however, was not the time for a debate. "Yes, us," I said. "Come on."

Adam muttered a few choice words, followed by, "I like normal rules. I like things like justice and clearly obvious bad guys and the rule of law and, well, basic physics. Footprints staying where they should be, that kind of thing. I like—"

"Hush!" I said, and thankfully he did.

"Maddie," I said, "we could do with your glamouring skills right now."

"Everyone stop," she said. There was a wobble in her voice and I reached out to give her hand a quick squeeze.

"You all right?"

"Yeah, sure. It's just … working with the Tylwyth Teg has been difficult lately, I don't know why."

"We all have our ups and downs," I said. "Do your best."

I could feel the tug of power that surrounded her as she called upon the skills of the Faerie Folk. She hummed under her breath, a strange plaintive song, but all of a sudden she choked and staggered against me.

"They won't come!" she said, staring at me in horror. She grabbed me. "They say I've broken the agreement! Bron, I haven't! I don't understand!"

She was utterly bereft and shaking. I wondered how it would feel if I could no longer ride the hedge; I'd be devastated. "Try again?" I hazarded.

She was crying. "They said no! They said I'd forgotten my duties to them! But Bron, I've sung to them in the garden every day, I've left them bread and milk and beer, what else would I do? Sian didn't tell me. She should have known, she said she knew…" Her voice was rising in hysteria.

"It's okay, it's okay," I said to her and I knew that it was not okay.

It was totally my fault.

I had taken the food because I didn't think the Faerie were in our garden.

Obviously they were. But now was not the time to open that can of worms, though. I gave her a light shake. I'd confess and pay penance later. "Maddie! They are tricksy. It's just another test, okay? It's just another test to see if you are really committed to them…"

Her eyes shone. "No, surely…"

I lied like our lives depended on it, which they did. "I am sure that Sian has told you everything that she can tell you. But remember in the old tales, how they test the loyalty of their devotees? That's all it is. Stay strong."

She sniffed but she was calmer. "But you need me."

"We can do this," I said. "Oh Maddie, I am sorry." I meant for everything that she didn't yet know about.

I let her go. She rubbed her face and wiped her nose, and

straightened up. She nodded slightly at me. "Let's carry on. Perhaps we can creep up on him."

Yeah, three people wearing colourful outdoor clothes could definitely hide in the middle of a featureless sea of white snow.

We had managed to get to twenty feet away when our luck ran out. Tait was following the path of the circle and as he rounded the far curve he saw us, and stopped dead, for one instant.

So did we.

Chloe noticed his sudden stop, and looked up at him, and followed his line of sight. As she turned her head, he leaped, and grabbed her in a bear hug from behind, clamping her tightly against him. She squeaked briefly, and then sagged in his arms.

Adam rushed forward and we followed, but Tait yelled out, "You stop right there now!"

Adam put out his hands and continued to walk forwards, but slowly now. Maddie and I flanked him like magical bodyguards.

Tait yelled out, desperation choking his voice. "I said stop! Or I will kill her. And then myself. So we will be together, see, anyway. You might as well let us go."

"Now listen, Edmund," Adam said, in a low and calming tone of voice that he'd probably learned on a police training course. "We're not here to judge you but you know we can't let you go, don't you? Don't you really want this all to end? We can help you. You don't really want to hurt Chloe…"

"Well, I'm not going to hurt her, am I? I'll keep her safe, by me always. Quick and painless, see." Tait shifted his weight and

Chloe was shoved to one side, so that he held her, still firmly, in his left arm. His right hand dipped into a pocket on his long green jacket, and emerged with a sinister flash of metal.

A knife.

He pressed it to her neck. "It's the kindest way," he said. "I won't let her bleed to death. I do it right, you know, quick-like. Like the sheep and the cattle. I know what I'm about, see. And we'll be together in the afterlife, at least, if you don't let us be together now. This is none of your business, none of you. Now go!"

We had all frozen in place as soon as we saw the knife. Adam looked at me, briefly, his eyes flicking frantically between my face, and the horrible tableau before us.

Chloe seemed to have woken from whatever dream-spell had been holding her. She was staring at us, her eyes huge, tears running down her face. She was shaking, trembling, her legs almost unable to support her. Tait was having to hold her up.

"Oh god," I whispered to Adam, as low as I possibly could. "He will do it, you know. He really will. He *believes*."

I saw Maddie nod out of the corner of my eye. Adam was a few inches behind us. He put his hands out and stopped either of us moving any further forward.

"Turn around," he whispered. "Take a step or two as if we are slowly going away."

We all faced the other way. "I don't like not watching," I said. "What's he doing?"

Maddie glanced back. "Just staring at us."

"I need to try to call for back-up again," he said. "I'm just not hopeful that Pol will believe me properly, or get anyone up here quickly enough once I do convince her. So what are we going to do?"

It unsettled me that a policeman was asking for help but he was right. We were in the realm of magic now. The problem was, we were all still human and awfully fallible.

I dragged in a breath and held it for a moment, feeling a renewed flood of energy spark right down to my fingertips. Power was rolling in me, and it came from many places: Gruffydd sent his strength, and Dilys her cunning, and Harkin sent his tenacity and slyness. From Maddie I drew deep friendship and love, from Horatio steadfast faith and wisdom, and from Adam there was – I blushed. Love, here, too. And from the land there was stability and from the storm there was passion. My ancestors hovered around and other spirits, nameless ones, looked on.

I *could do this*.

But I could not do everything.

Whatever I did, I would have to focus with the whole of my being.

I glanced back at them. Tait was glaring at us and he waved the knife in the air when he saw me looking. We didn't have long to make a decision.

"Guys, listen," I said. "I can go and save her … I am sure of it. But that leaves you two here exposed to anything, I don't know what … but we know he won't give her up easily."

"That's a no-brainer," Maddie said. "We can save ourselves. You go, we're the backup for you now, right? Anyway, I have the Tylwyth Teg on my side."

I didn't think they were on anyone's side, not even hers at this moment, but she believed, and so I let it lie. "If it goes wrong..." I started to say.

"If it goes wrong, it goes wrong. You don't get guarantees. But we are with you."

Adam said, "Do what you have to do."

TWENTY-FOUR

I gripped the loops of my backpack where they fitted around the front of my shoulders, acknowledged all the sources of power and insight that were around me and within me, and spun around to face Tait and Chloe. Adam and Maddie took a few steps back, away from the scene, and I began to stride forward decisively.

Tait held the knife high in the air and screamed at me in Welsh, then English. "Don't you come anywhere near me, don't you dare now!"

Chloe sagged against his arm and he had to shift his weight to catch her. The knife stayed in his hand but he couldn't use it; he wanted to keep Chloe on her feet but she seemed to have completely fainted. By fear or by magic, I could not tell.

So I kept on walking forward until I was just ten feet away from him, and I stumbled as I came slap-bang up against a protection he had cast around them. Or maybe it came from the stone circle itself. Certainly there was power there, humming up from the stones which were invisible, buried deep in the snow.

I put out my hands and placed them against the solid air that surrounded him, feeling for a way in. He had drawn on the energy of the earth and it was neither good nor bad; it simply was. I asked for entry, neutrally and politely, and it parted for me.

He let Chloe crumple to the ground but as she fell, still unconscious, she caught the knife with her heavy coat sleeve and it was knocked from his hand. He whirled around and put his hands up to me, like an old-school boxer.

"I am warning you now!" he yelled. "I will call down the terrors of the night upon you, I will!"

"I *am* the terrors of the night," I told him, and a little thrill went through me that I'd managed to come up with something that sounded pretty cool. I hoped that Adam had heard it.

And that it didn't put him off me being his girlfriend and all that.

"You have no idea what I can bring down here at my will!" Tait called.

He put his hands to the sky then, and tipped his head back, and he howled with an intensity that made my spine tingle. He was like a madman, like a wolf, like a screaming banshee.

I hesitated, and it was my undoing. I should have run forward before he completed his spell but I wanted to be sure what I was running into.

The thing is, sometimes you *can't* be sure, and yet you have to act regardless.

I didn't act.

That second was all he needed. Then there were hoof beats and I thought for a moment it was only the Wild Hunt – only! As if they were safe! – but it was not the Hunt, not at all, nothing like. There were teeth, great white slabs like gravestones and there was hair, black and thick and matted with blood, and there was muscle like rocks and ropes.

He howled in triumph, falling to his knees, and I saw rear above him a great black horse with shining red eyes and an expression of fury and damnation.

It was the pwca, and like a blow to my stomach I realised how David Hudson had died.

And the key to it all was in my backpack.

I shrugged it free from my shoulders and fought for the zip which eluded my shaking hands and thick gloved fingers. I pawed at it, not daring to take my eyes from the pwca before me. I could smell it, and that shocked me. This was a beast of the otherworld yet it smelled of broken bones and carcases and rotting, abandoned farmyards.

I pulled at the backpack and it burst open, the zip splitting and I tipped it all to the snow, letting the jars and bags and a notebook land in a heap. I knew what I needed and I risked a quick glance, just long enough to spot and grab the tangle of horsehair that Chloe had given me.

It was not a good gift. But it was the gift that I needed.

This was the bridle made of three hairs of the pwca's tail, and it was with this that I could tame the spirit. Dean had sung of it.

I held it up and stared that beast right in the eyes. It looked back at me. The gaze burned and made me feel sick but I held on. It had to realise that I not only had the thing in my hands that could be used to tame it, but I had the power to hold it, once tamed, too.

I braced my legs at shoulder-width apart, and bellowed the first challenging thing that rose in my mind.

It wasn't my best line.

"Come on then!"

But hell, it worked, and the pwca came.

Tait was still howling and he ran after the pwca but no one would ever outrun the shape-changing-horse-spirit-beast-thing.

I began to sing the song that Dean had taught me, and I dropped my gloves to the ground so I could untangle the horsehairs. I had a hazy idea of what a rough bridle should look like. I fashioned it into a halter, with one long loop to go over the cheeks and around the ears, and the other loop to go around the nose. Then I held it aloft while the pwca circled me.

It did a wide turn and went behind Adam and Maddie, its piston-like legs powering into the snow. Sometimes it touched the ground when it leaped, and sometimes it was in mid-air, stepping on nothing at all.

I had a clear aim. In a flash, quicker than thought itself, I acted, at last. I could not afford not to, or the beast would destroy me. As the pwca danced towards me, with Tait coming up behind me, I lunged to its sinister head and flung the bridle up and onto its long nose with my left hand. My right hand fumbled for and grabbed the long loop, as I leaped up into the air and tried to wrestle it over the pwca's ears.

The beast felt greasy and hot to my touch, but spirits guided me and I managed to get the loop in the right place. Perhaps it was always going to cleave to its home. And it was all I needed to do – like with Gruffydd and his horse, I found myself almost catapulted into the air and onto the pwca's back.

I had done it.

I was dizzy with exhilaration.

Tait looked like he was a long way down, beneath us. Partly that was the sheer height of the horse, and partly that was because we were now prancing a foot above the snow. I almost giggled as the pwca's terrifying power infused me. I could get used to this. Something was picking at my brain, encouraging me to feel the energy, abandon my morals, my ethics, my day to day humdrum concerns – *life could be like this all the time*, the pwca told me, hissing in my head. *Just ride, let's just ride*, it said. *Such abandon! Doesn't this feel so good? So right?*

"I don't listen to the Tylwyth Teg and I certainly don't listen to you," I told it, speaking out loud. "Go on!"

I didn't know how to steer it, so I forced it with my will alone. I focused on Chloe, ahead of us in the snow. She was coming back to consciousness again, and weakly raising herself up on one arm, looking our way. I intended to get to her before Tait decided to turn around and finish what he had threatened to do earlier.

The pwca reared up, its front legs pawing the air. Then it plunged forwards and I was thrown back, but somehow – magically, is all I can assume – I remained on it, my hands knotted in its repellent mane.

And from behind me, I heard a scream, short and strangled and cut off.

I twisted, and saw Maddie in a crumpled heap, a bloom of

red already spreading in the snow around her, and Adam was on his knees, urgently pulling at her. The rear legs of the pwca had kicked out and caught her a blow. I called out but the words were pulled from my mouth by cold air rushing in.

Tait was screaming, too, the howling cry of a man who had lost his mind, long ago. He chanted something and I had no idea what he was calling up, but it could not bode well.

And Chloe was struggling to her feet.

And still the pwca tried to convince me that I could ride away from all this, and be free.

No.

I made another choice.

I jumped down from its back.

TWENTY-FIVE

I landed in the snow, and miraculously stayed on my feet with just a wobble, my arms windmilling. The pwca wheeled around and faced me, its mad eyes rolling. Tait came clawing towards us, gasping.

The pwca was now the one who was hesitating.

"Go!" I bellowed to it. "The power is yours. Take it and go!"

It danced.

"No!" Tait screamed, and he pushed past me, reaching out to the pwca.

The pwca called to me silently. *"Come with me."*

"Go," I yelled back at it.

It came towards me. Tait reached for it but it shouldered him aside and turned, putting itself between me and the farmer. It bent its head to me and I realised what I still had to do.

"You are released," I said, over and over, as I undid the knots of the horsehair bridle, picking at them frantically. The strands fell away, uncurling as they fell. I snatched them back up. They could easily be woven anew. I thrust my hand out to the pwca. "You are released!"

It snuffled my hand, its breath rancid and then, so gently, it took the three strands between its massive teeth.

I just had time to throw myself backwards as it reared up again, and then it turned around.

Tait, still howling out a meaningless, animal stream of noise, plunged through the snow after it, but his boots slipped. I ran, and jumped, and landed on his back like a monkey, my hands clawing for a hold. I got an arm around his neck and tried to squeeze, hoping to choke him enough to get him to the ground.

But he was big and strong and filled with anger. He didn't fall to the ground like I'd hoped.

And then someone else joined the fray, launching themselves onto his flailing left arm. I heard a crack and a crunch, and there was long blonde hair in my face. It was Chloe, roused from her stupor, and wreaking vengeance on the man who had wronged her. It leant her a strength I could not hope to match. But I applied renewed force and together we brought him down to the ground.

Maybe I had used a little too much pressure on his neck. He twitched, and then lay still.

I sat back on my heels, my heart pounding, and looked across at Chloe who was still beating at his arm and upper back with her fists, tears falling.

"It's over," I told her gently.

She wept and collapsed forwards, and then the dusky twilight was lit by strobes of blue.

TWENTY-SIX

Sergeant Polly Jones herself had come out in a police car, some big Range Rover type of thing, and it was parked a distance away on the track, but the lights carried through the night. She had been promoted way beyond her competence, and if I were feeling uncharitable, I'd say her competency level was around the level of tea-maker. Still, she was technically in charge and she bounced her way through the snowy field. She made walking look harder work than it was. She had a radio clamped to her ear, and was waving her other arm in the air.

Trekking along behind her was a quad bike with Gordon from Blue Hill Farm riding on it, flanked to one side by an open-mouthed collie dog, its tongue lolling out. The quad was moving slowly and leading two stocky figures in orange who I assumed were from the mountain rescue team. They would be busy today, I reckoned.

To my relief, Maddie was on her feet and Adam called one of the orange-clad people to her, a stocky woman who gathered Maddie up and began to talk to her.

Adam and Pol came over to me. I got to my feet and stood

next to Chloe. We looked down at the prostrate Tait lying motionless in the snow. I felt slightly guilty.

"He's not dead," I offered with a nervous laugh. I was pretty sure he wasn't dead, anyway. He didn't feel very dead. No spirit or shade was hanging around the body.

Adam knelt down and set about the basic first-on-scene procedures. He looked up at me. "Well done," he said. "No, he's not *quite* dead."

At that, Tait began to stir. Then he thrashed around a bit, gurgling, and I stepped back with Chloe to my side. Adam calmed him down and then Pol read him his rights as she arrested him. It didn't seem to make much of an impression on him. They got him to his feet and began to walk him to the police car.

Chloe stepped forward. I put out my hand. "Wait," I said. "You need to be seen too."

"I'm fine. Aren't I being…"

"What?"

She turned to me and she was almost as white as the snow. She shivered. "Arrested?"

"What for? You didn't ask to be kidnapped by that man. Don't let him mess with your head. It's all over now." I nodded towards the little gathering around Maddie. "Come on, let's get you sorted."

Chloe walked alongside me, stumbling. A crushing weariness was beginning to settle on me, too. I needed food, I needed drink, I desperately needed a wee, and I really really *really* wanted a nice warm bed for, oh, about thirty hours.

"Bron, listen," she said, bumping against me, and pulling at my arm. "He did it for me."

"I know, but that's not your fault," I said.

But a sick feeling was forming in my stomach. There was yet more to this tale than I fully understood.

"I didn't realise how Edmund felt about me," Chloe went on. "I am so sorry. I should not have given the pwca's bridle to you."

"You knew what it was?"

"I did. Because it was me that gave it to Edmund in the first place."

I stopped walking. We were just out of earshot of the mountain rescue people and Maddie, but they were looking at us, expecting us to continue.

"Why did you give it to him? Did you know what he was going to do with it?" I hissed.

She hung her head. "We just wanted to scare him out of the way."

"We? But this makes no sense. You wanted to be together…?"

"No." She was sobbing now. "Edmund's always been my friend, you know. A good friend of the family. Even when I went off to college and then to work, he stayed in touch, and I knew he was the one person I could always rely on. So it was really important to me that he and David–" her voice choked on his name. "I wanted him and David to get on together. But they didn't. David had always been quite intense, you know? I loved his passion, his drive. But his fits of temper got worse when we came back here. He was so strong and protective that it made

221

me feel really loved, but then, after a while, I started to see that he wasn't protecting me in a nice way. He was possessing me and that's different. I got scared. And every time I tried to talk about it with him, he got angry. I didn't want to upset him."

"You didn't want to upset him, but you got Tait to kill him?"

"No! That wasn't supposed to happen. David didn't like it here. He wanted to leave but I feel safe here. So we wanted to scare him away, you know, just make him go. My family had the pwca's bridle from way back and I gave it to Edmund and told him what it would do. He tested it out and I think he liked it."

I remembered the feeling of dizzying wild abandon. Yes, I could have got used to that feeling too. It was intoxicating. "And then what?"

"The day that David died, we'd all been together in the new shop. Edmund and David went off, and I told them I'd follow soon. It was the plan, you see. Edmund got David alone and called the pwca and they all got swept up. But David fell."

"Was he pushed?" I said.

"No, no," she replied.

"Listen, think. Knowing what you know now – that Tait really has a thing for you, something he thinks he's entitled to – can you be absolutely sure that he wasn't pushed?"

She covered her face with her hands, and I knew that she suspected the same thing that I suspected – that Tait had pushed David from a great height. Did he intend to kill him? Judging by Tait's current mental state, we would perhaps never truly know.

"What are they going to do to me?" she mumbled through her fingers. "I am an accomplice to murder."

"I don't know. I should tell you to tell the truth but I'm not entirely sure they'd believe you."

Maddie and the woman in orange were approaching us now, evidently tired of waiting for us. Chloe's tale was lost in a flurry of "how are you" and "oh my god" and "glad that's over" and "let's get home."

The police car had already disappeared, taking Tait to a cell somewhere. Was he going to confess? If he did, he'd sound quite mad. As for Chloe, I didn't know what to do about her at all. Adam had gone, and it was Pol Jones who was left on the scene, frantically talking in her radio once again.

What did we have here? Just an abduction, I realised, and now it was over.

I fell against Maddie and we hugged tightly, and allowed ourselves to be led to the road where there were four-wheel-drive vehicles now waiting, lodged in the snow at odd angles, their headlights illuminating the eerie night.

***

"I love you guys," I said, and collapsed onto the rug in front of the range in the once-again warm and toasty kitchen.

Lacey sneered until she noticed that I really was close to actually passing out. Then all three of them rushed to my aid, collecting Maddie as she stumbled into the room too, and we were surrounded by a high-pitched, energetic and highly efficient triple teenage whirlwind.

"Dilys?" I croaked as a hot water bottle was pressed to my

belly and my boots were stripped from my feet. Chloe had been dropped off at her parents' farm.

Gruffydd was there, then, kneeling between us both. "I heard from the hospital and she'll be fine but they're keeping her overnight for observation."

"Oh no," I said.

"It's the best place for her," he reassured me.

"No, I mean, those poor nurses." I'd send them chocolates once their ordeal was over. And thinking of chocolates made my stomach grumble. When had I last eaten? That energy gel and a few biscuits didn't count. I waved at the dresser on the side. "Lower left cupboard."

Kelly darted over and pulled out a carrier bag. She looked inside, and then at all of us, her eyebrows raised.

"Yes," I said, weakly. What we all needed now was sugar and fat and caffeine and indulgence, I'd decided. Clean eating? Pah. "Hand them all out. Everyone."

"It's not Easter yet."

"But it *is* the equinox. It is Eostre," I said. "And you've all earned it."

Maddie said, "So have you."

And we feasted on the chocolate eggs and rabbits until everything went black and sleep claimed me and I woke up from time to time in my own bed. Sometimes I smiled, and turned over, and went back to sleep, remembering that I was home and safe.

And sometimes I remembered how I'd caused Maddie to fall out of favour with the Faerie, and I needed to atone for that, and I lay awake for a little while, worrying in the darkness.

224

TWENTY-SEVEN

Adam brought Dilys home to us the next morning. Maddie flew around her, her warmth enveloping Dilys and I stepped back. Maddie's talents were what she needed right now. Dilys wanted to wash the "stink of the hospital" from her and Maddie helped her upstairs to run a bath. Harkin followed, to perform his usual role of keeping an eye on her in the bathroom.

I poured a cup of tea for Adam and we sat at the table. He looked at me carefully.

"What are the roads like?" I asked him first.

He rolled his eyes. "You lot. So British. Weather and traffic. Yeah, the main roads are all passable. The temperature's rising quickly and the snow won't last. It was just a freak snowfall."

"We have them every year."

"Freaks are pretty common," he said.

"Excuse me?"

"You know what I mean." He reached out and took both my hands in one of his. "It is a good thing. You are a good thing. And you were very brave last night."

"Adam… have you spoken with Chloe?"

"Not yet. It will take her a while to get over this but we can refer her to some specialist support services."

"Right." I needed to tread carefully. "Okay, what about Tait? Has he spoken about David Hudson at all?"

"He has ranted about him."

"Has he said that he killed him?"

"He has said that he wanted to, but it's not a confession. He didn't make a lot of sense."

"I can't believe he might get away with it!" I said, and clenched my fists. Adam patted down on my hands.

"He won't," he said. "Anyway, he's definitely going to be charged with kidnapping and perhaps false imprisonment. Both of those offences carry a life sentence."

"I hope he confesses," I said. "It matters. I didn't like what I saw of David Hudson but his death matters, even so."

I took a deep breath, then, and told Adam what Chloe had told me, ending with, "So you see, she isn't innocent."

"Ah. Well, if Tait confesses and mentions her then we will take it further. I just don't see it holding up in court. Flying horse-things? No, it will be laughed away, I'm afraid."

"It's not justice," I said.

"Is it not? Do you want to see Chloe spend time in prison?"

I sighed and flattened out my hands. "No, I suppose not."

"We'll wait and see what Tait reveals," he said. "Some kind of justice will be done, I promise you that."

"Thank you."

"You look exhausted."

"Thanks again."

"Seriously. You should go back to bed. You've got nothing else important to do today, have you?"

"Actually," I said, "I have. There is one thing still that's not come home yet."

***

It was midday. The back door to the utility room stood open and so did the door between that room and the kitchen. Cool air wafted in.

I sat at one long edge of the scrubbed wooden table and Maddie sat opposite me. Dilys had taken her place at the head of the table, wrapped in shawls.

I was tired. I had risen early to prepare for this, and also to make my amends with the Tylwyth Teg. I had gone out, feeling rather nervous about dealing with them, and made as much of an offering as I felt I could. I'd even sung to them. I heard far off laughter and knew that I had to confess to Maddie, too.

I hadn't done so yet.

Then I had communed with Rhiannon and she had stroked a gentle warm hand down the back of my neck, and I heard birdsong, and I realised that everything I did for a bird of the air, I did for her, and it was all going to be alright. There was balance.

Finally, we had this last thing to do.

Three candles burned in the middle of the table, surrounded by a hastily-constructed wreath of ivy and early spring flowers I'd gathered from the garden. There was also some newly-made bread, still warm and slightly damp, and half a glass of foaming beer.

Something rustled in the utility room. I'd left the cages open and things had returned, if they were able to, rounded up by Harkin.

We held hands and Dilys began to speak in Welsh. I caught fragments of her words, but I knew the intention and that was the thing that mattered. Maddie didn't understand a thing but again, she too knew what we were about.

We called the spirits of the house back home.

We sang, in our own way, in our own words, of the hearth and the stone. Of the fire at the centre and the walls that surround. We wove ourselves together and within and let the genii loci come back to its place once more.

You can't describe a magic spell, really, you know. I can set down the words and the actions but the actual intent behind it is the thing that really counts. All the ritual parts are just ways of altering one's consciousness enough to bend reality – such as you might conceive it – to your will. Or, perhaps better, to seek a way of working with that reality towards the aim that you want.

The house breathed in. And sighed out, and settled.

We were home.

***

A few days later I was walking through the town centre. There was no sign of the snow. It had gone by the following evening and now everything smelled of spring again. The pots outside the shops in the market square were bright green with the emerging shoots of bulbs and already the crocuses were in full bloom. I'd dropped off some lunch at Sian's shop. Maddie had been in a hurry and forgotten to take anything to eat. I'd even, in a rare spirit of charitable feeling, taken an extra piece of cake to give to Sian.

Sian sent Maddie into the back room for something vague when I entered. "Thank you for the cake," she said. "Have you thought about my proposal?"

"Yes. Is it a secret from Maddie?"

"No, not at all! I just didn't want her to feel odd about me asking you."

"She wouldn't. Don't be daft." In truth I thought that Sian was just the type who liked secrets for holding a secret's sake. Anything that smacked of power over another. That was what it was all about, in the end, for her.

Don't second guess people's intentions, Horatio had warned me.

"What's your timescale on the retreat?" I asked.

"I have premises and a few other tutors lined up. This summer," she said, "at the very latest. I will do a trial run soon with some friends as dummy punters. So you're on board?"

I meant to say no. I really did. But maybe the Tylwyth Teg were having their revenge on me because there was a distant ringing and singing and suddenly I was saying, "Yes, of course."

I staggered out of the shop feeling slightly violated.

I had confessed my sins to Maddie a little while earlier, and she had been horrified, upset, and most painfully of all, disappointed with me. It had taken a lot of apologising to get beyond that, but I had done, in the end. I assured her I'd acted impulsively and from the best of intentions.

She had grudgingly accepted that.

But I had known there would be a reckoning and that it wouldn't come from Maddie.

Now I was wandering and feeling slightly aimless. I waved to Lacey who was perched on a bench with only Eira at her side. She half waved back, but she didn't look like she wanted to talk to me. On the opposite side of the square was another group of young people, boys and girls, and she was watching them.

That was not my world.

Still, she was emerging into adulthood and she might yet do that babysitting I'd asked her about. And in return, would I teach her, as she had requested?

I should get her to go on Sian's retreat, I thought viciously. What was I even going to talk about?

I put it from my mind. Maybe it would never happen.

As I pottered on, mercifully thinking of very little, a car rolled up alongside me, making me jump. "Hey!" Adam called from the rolled-down window.

"Are you on shift?" I asked.

"Not yet. I'm early. Fancy grabbing a drink?"

"Brandy please."

"Nope."

"Oh, all right. Caffi Cwtch?"

"I'll park and see you there," he said. "You know what I like."

And I did, and that felt nice. I ordered a large coffee for him and a sticky Danish pastry with icing on it, that was probably no closer to Denmark's traditional food than the *bara brith* I'd bought for myself.

Alston sneered as Adam entered, looking him up and down sourly. "Well, that's my business gone for the day," he commented. "Does me no good to have a uniform in here. Puts people right off."

I ignored him and took the tray to a far table where we could people-watch through the big windows. Adam slid onto a chair bedecked with pink gingham and frills, and dropped his hat onto the chair next to him. "So," he said, without preamble. "Tait's in hospital."

"Still?"

"No, a new one. Psychiatric. He needs help."

"Ah. Oh." I felt sorry for him, after all that. The pwca had messed with his head. Although I suspected his head was half-messed in the first place. Still, you wouldn't wish any kind of illness, mental or otherwise, on anyone. "So what will happen now?"

"I am not sure and it's not down to me. We've done our bit and it's really out of our hands. The Crown Prosecution Service go from here. But he will be detained, one way or the other. That will have to be enough."

In a funny way, it was. "And Chloe?"

"I've been to see her. It was an awkward conversation," he said with a rueful laugh. "I tried to ask subtle questions about a matter that I only half-understand and only quarter believe."

"You do believe what I told you?" I said, urgently.

"Yes. I believe everything you tell me," he said. "It's just really hard to talk about in a way that sounds like I believe."

"I know. Thank you. So what will happen to her?"

"Nothing. She has suffered. You know Hudson used to get physically violent with her? She's been hospitalised twice."

"Oh, god." I recoiled. "The monster."

"Quite. She's planning a fresh start. She will move away, back to where she has friends in London. She seems racked by guilt, so there is her punishment. It will follow her for ever. And in a funny way, that's worse. She doesn't get the closure of a punishment that she thinks she deserves. But I suspect her only crime was foolishness."

"To stay with Hudson?"

"No, to believe Tait, to get caught up with him. As for staying with Hudson, even though he abused her, that's a whole different world and she is not to blame, you know."

"I suppose not." *I'd walk away,* I thought.

But I felt sad. No. Would I? Walking away is hard. Harder than people think.

"Hey, don't be down about it," Adam said.

"No, it's not that," I replied. "I was thinking about how hard it is to walk away from things."

He took a few gulps of his coffee. "Ask Maddie about that," he said. "She came a long way to get here."

"She came a long way to get home," I said. The sadness ached at me and I knew its cause.

"Hey, are you eating that?" he asked, glancing at his watch.

I pushed half of the speckled fruit bread across to him. "Help yourself. Don't be late for your shift."

He grabbed the cake, kissed me, and left in a hurry.

***

I didn't want to go home. I thought about walking away, about what I needed to do. Maddie was discovering her place here and it was wonderful, if a little scary. And Dilys was getting older.

My problems, my effect on technology, were causing too many issues. If Dilys was losing out on getting bookings, because of me, then that had to change. And Maddie had to go out of the house to contact her folks in America, or wait for me to leave, and even then my lingering presence hampered her efforts.

I'd discovered what Dilys had been hiding under her shawl, and the subject of her hidden, hurried, whispered conversations with Maddie. She'd acquired a "tablet" which turned out to be the shiny black rectangle thing I'd seen on the table. It was like Maddie's iPad and they had been trying to use it to get online while I was out of the house. But my influence was so melded into the fabric of the house that it had not been successful.

So the obvious solution was the hardest one. I needed to move out.

I was in my late twenties, for heaven's sake. Some people had been married a decade by now, with kids, and jobs, and responsibilities. Here I was, worrying about nothing, not compared to them.

Yet walking away was hard.

I wouldn't leave Llanfair, I knew that. It wasn't going to be the same kind of transatlantic wrench that Maddie had done. And now I was committed to helped Sian with her new plan. So getting my own flat should have been exciting. But I'd be leaving my ancestral home, my garden, and the spirits of the place I'd grown up in.

I quickened my pace. It was a sacrifice I had to make.

There was always a reckoning.

I thought I heard a distant laughter, but it wasn't the Faerie this time. It wasn't quite so malevolent.

If I had to swear to it, I'd have said it sounded like Horatio.

Also available:

All Cats Are Grey In The Dark

The third volume following the magical mystery adventures of Bron the Welsh hedge witch, her American cousin Maddie and their crazy bunch of friends (and enemies).

Herbs are good for you, right?

Maybe not so good for one person - who's found dead beside a cauldron of magical herbs. Glittery, frilly Sian Pederi is running a course up in the hills called "Unfurl Your Inner Spirit" and it's all path working, ley lines, drumming and vegan food ... until the corpse rocks up.

Bron needs to get to the bottom of it, but literally everyone wanted this person dead – and even Bron herself could have cheerfully hit them with a tree branch.

She's got other problems, too. Harkin, her cat, is obsessed with the number three. Her mad Great Aunt might, or might not, be plotting the demise of her actual nemesis Elsie Delaney and hunky police officer Adam is being just so impossibly nice.

With more Celtic folklore, faeries, druids, helpful vicars, London journalists and random hippies than you can shake an authentic hand-carved sigil-adorned harp at ... welcome back to the crazy world of Llanfair!

If you enjoyed this book, please leave a review! It really helps. Thank you.

Made in United States
Orlando, FL
04 December 2023

40158031R00143